"DAMN! WHAT A MESS!"

Longarm knew that he wasn't going to be able to grab the lines, and he doubted that he could leap on the back of the nearest horse and try to pull it to a stop, but there didn't seem to be any choice but to try.

Here goes, he thought, jumping.

Somehow, he did land on the back of the wheel horse, and then he grabbed the lines and started wrenching on them. The stage began to slow but not before they careened into that sharp right turn. Longarm decided that the coach was not going to make it. He could feel the coach lean precariously toward the steep drop-off into a canyon, and he bellowed, "It's going over! Jump!"

And then, because he was a firm believer in taking his own good advice, Longarm also jumped.

TABOR EVANS

LONGARM

AND
THE GRAVE ROBBERS

JOVE BOOKS, NEW YORK

LONGARM AND THE GRAVE ROBBERS

A Jove Book / published by arrangement with the author

PRINTING HISTORY
Jove edition / November 1998

All rights reserved.
Copyright © 1998 by Jove Publications, Inc.
This book may not be reproduced in whole or in part, by mimeograph or any other means, without permission. For information address:
The Berkley Publishing Group, a member of Penguin Putnam Inc., 375 Hudson Street, New York, New York 10014.

The Penguin Putnam Inc. World Wide Web site address is http://www.penguinputnam.com

ISBN: 0-515-12392-7

A JOVE BOOK®
Jove Books are published by The Berkley Publishing Group, a member of Penguin Putnam Inc.,
375 Hudson Street, New York, New York 10014.
JOVE and the "J" design are trademarks belonging to Jove Publications, Inc.

PRINTED IN THE UNITED STATES OF AMERICA

10 9 8 7 6 5 4 3 2 1

Chapter 1

"Custis, I have a tough job for you this time," United States Marshal Billy Vail said, looking grim.

Deputy Marshal Custis Long scowled and took a seat in his boss's office located in Denver's Federal Building. He considered propping his boots up on the edge of Billy's desk, then rejected the idea. He and Billy were good and longtime friends, but he did work for the man.

"A tough job," Longarm repeated. "Billy, *all* the jobs that you give me are tough. Why should I expect that this one would be any different?"

"No reason, I guess," Billy said, steepling his short, thick fingers and rearranging papers on his desk.

Stout and pudgy, Billy was a direct contrast to Longarm. But Billy's eyes were sharp, and even if he was lacking in stature, there was nothing wrong with the quality of his brain. Billy was bright and Longarm respected the man, although he could be trying at times.

"Custis, I got a long letter from the town of Cortez this morning, and they've got a rather unusual problem over in the old Anasazi country around the Four Corners area.''

''Rough country, that.''

''Yeah, isn't it, though. I remember one time I was chasing a gang of . . . aw, never mind. There's no time for me to spin old stories.''

''I *enjoy* your stories,'' Custis assured the man. ''It's just that I've heard them all about ten or twelve times.''

''Aw, get outa here!''

''Well, maybe only four or five times each then,'' Longarm said, thinking how easy it was to pull Billy's string and get him flustered.

In his younger days, Billy had been a field man himself before being promoted to a desk job. And although he made a lot more money now, he still considered those times when he'd been a deputy marshal his happiest. However, when a man took on a wife and a family, he needed to be more settled, and that was what Billy had chosen to be for the second half of his law career.

''The thing of it is,'' Billy continued, ''I *do* know that Four Corners country and it *is* wild. There's a lot of outlaws running lose over there on the far side of the Rocky Mountains and—''

''And you're sending me in there to clean 'em out single-handed. Right?''

''No,'' Billy said, ''not unless you've got a little extra time on your hands. The job I have for you probably involves some of 'em, though. But what we have out there is an organized band of Anasazi grave robbers.''

''Don't—''

''Let me finish,'' Billy said. ''Custis, as you probably know, the Anasazi people were most likely the ancestors of the Hopi, Zuni, and who knows who else. They built pueblos and those big cliff dwellings at Mesa Verde.''

"Never have had the time to see them," Longarm said. "Always too much of a hurry. But I've heard that they are an amazing sight."

"You can be sure of that," Billy told him. "And I promise that you'll have the chance on this trip to see the Mesa Verde cliff dwellings because the letter on my desk is from a Miss Candice Mason. She claims that grave robbers in the Four Corners are thicker'n lice and they're looting Anasazi artifacts and selling them to a ring of international thieves."

"Do you believe that, or do you think she's just another one of them old biddies that have nothing better to do than cry wolf every time she sees an Indian pot or arrowhead?"

"I believe her," Billy said, "because I know Candice. Or at least, I knew her mother. They're a good, solid ranching family. The girl's mother died a few years back and *she* was a treasure in that part of the country. A real Florence Nightingale. Candice's late father was a state legislator and also highly respected."

"How old is Candice?"

"I don't know. Maybe in her early twenties. I've heard that she runs the old homestead ranch and is doing pretty well at it too."

"All right," Longarm said, "so she's not crying wolf."

"I want you to go there and investigate. We have a rich Anasazi heritage here in Colorado, and damned if I want a bunch of profiteers and looters to be capitalizing on it."

"All right," Longarm said. "Actually, I've heard that American Indians have been the rage in Europe ever since Buffalo Bill Cody took his Wild West Show over there a few years back."

"That's right. And Mesa Verde is just one of the sites of old Anasazi ruins located in southeastern Colorado. According to Miss Mason, there are hundreds, probably thousands more throughout the entire region. This telegram says that some of the locals have tried to protect them from the looters and have been shot for their interference."

"Is this a *federal* problem, or a local one?"

"It's federal if they are transporting old Indian bones, pots, and whatever else they can traffic in across state lines. The last thing we want is our nation's heritage going overseas to European curiosity shops or museums."

"I suppose you're right."

"Of course I am," Billy said. "And Miss Mason says that the Indians down there are so upset they're starting to take things into their own hands. Innocent people might be killed. Hell, you could have all kinds of complications if the atmosphere gets sticky. Custis, unless we nip it in the bud, we could have an honest-to-goodness Indian war!"

"Oh," Longarm said, smothering a grin, "I think that might be stretching things a bit."

"How can you be sure? If someone was digging up the bones of your grandmother, for example, wouldn't you be upset enough to shed some blood?"

"Nah," Longarm said, keeping a straight face, "my grandmother was a regular old witch. Anybody who would fool with her remains would deserve 'em."

"Don't patronize me, Custis! This is real serious business. People are being killed. I know that for a fact. And I believe that Miss Mason is right to say that there is probably an organized gang dealing in Anasazi bones."

"What does that term mean?"

4

"What term?"

"Anasazi."

"It means something like 'the ancient ones,' if I remember correctly."

"Huh. Well, I guess that the next thing you'll say is that you want me to leave on the first train down to Pueblo."

"I do."

"Dammit, Billy, I just returned from Montana," Longarm complained, "and I'm a mite worn down. You promised me that I could have a few weeks of long-overdue vacation time, and I've sort of found a lady that would like me to share some time with her."

"There's always a lady who wants you to share time with her. This is important!"

"So is the lady."

"Yeah, well, the lady can wait."

"*You* tell her that," Longarm said.

"Listen, I know you've got a lot of vacation time coming, and I know that Montana thing was pretty rough. You did one hell of a job of there, and don't think that my superior doesn't know about it. Why, even the *governor* knows about it."

"Nice to hear that," Longarm said, "but I still need some time off."

"Look, I know I made you a promise," Billy said. "But this is a job that I don't want to give to anyone but you. It requires sensitivity to the Indians' feelings about the fate of their revered ancestors. When you get into the Four Corners area and start investigating things, you'll be walking a tightrope between the Indians and this gang of grave robbers."

"Why?" Longarm asked. "I'll just let the Indians know that I'm working in their behalf. That way—"

"That way you'll never catch the grave robbers or infiltrate their gang."

"You don't know that."

"Listen," Billy said, "Miss Mason says right here in this letter that the talk around Cortez is that this is a very sophisticated operation. It'd have to be, Custis! Otherwise, these people would be caught when they try to sell artifacts."

"Why? Seems to me that they could get away with that and not be caught."

"If they try to sell artifacts to legitimate museums or historical societies, they'll be red-flagged. It's against the law to loot Indian graves. No," Billy said, "I think that the Anasazi artifacts are probably flowing to San Francisco and New York, then being sold overseas to rich collectors. That means that the looters are far more organized and entrenched than just a few grave robbers skulking around deserted Indian ruins."

"Okay, Billy, I get the point. But what . . ."

"I won't be satisfied if all you do is nab a few grave diggers, Custis. I want you to infiltrate the entire gang and arrest the leaders of this organization. Clean it out from the top on down. We want to send a message to everyone out there that this practice might be lucrative, but it's also illegal as hell and will not be tolerated!"

Keeping a straight face, Longarm said, "Then it sounds like I'll probably have to follow a trail all the way to Europe or Singapore or some such place. I could do that."

"Don't be ridiculous! This department hasn't got *that* kind of money to be sending deputy marshals all over the world. And if it did, my boss would insist that *he* be the one that went to Europe or Asia, not you."

"Your boss couldn't find a mouse in a cheese factory,'' Longarm snorted with derision. ''And I'm starting to think that you've also lost your sense.''

''I don't know why I put up with you,'' Billy said, looking pained.

''You put up with me because I'm the best man on your payroll. But I won't be much longer if I don't start getting some recreation.''

''Recreation? Hell,'' Billy replied without a trace of sympathy, ''the last time we gave you a couple of weeks off, we got a telegram begging for money and help to get you out of a New Orleans jail! If we hadn't intervened on your behalf, you'd still be behind bars.''

''I was framed.''

Billy waved his hand in dismissal. ''I've heard that story about a dozen times and it always changes. The thing of it is, you *owe* me and your department a few favors.''

''I've repaid you over and over,'' Longarm replied, his smile slipping. ''And I'll do it again this time, but dammit, I want a *signed* letter stating that I will have a *month's* paid vacation starting the minute I return to Denver after clearing up this Anasazi business.''

''All right, if you don't trust me.''

''When it comes to time off, I don't trust you,'' Longarm told him.

''Suit yourself. I'll draft a letter and have it typed by Henry this morning. You'll get it when you pick up your travel money.''

''How much this time?'' Longarm asked. ''Or were you thinking of giving me the usual damned dollar-a-day pittance?''

''No, no,'' Billy said. ''Since it's nearing the end of the fiscal year and we have a surplus, I think we can give you . . . say, two dollars a day.''

7

"And a train ticket to Pueblo, a stage ticket from Pueblo to Cortez, and enough extra money to outfit myself with a horse, pack animal, and supplies."

"Christ," Billy swore, "you really want to go in style, don't you?"

"I don't mean to ride no damned burro after this gang, or be laughed at or thought a bum, that's for certain."

"I can advance you . . . a hundred dollars."

"I won't do it for less than a hundred and fifty plus the tickets," Longarm said stubbornly. "Last two times I've had to wire for money."

"And we sent it."

"Yeah, but it was a huge bother and it exposed me both times. I mean, when you're supposed to be someone other than a federal lawman, why would you telegraph the federal government for additional expense money?"

"Okay! One hundred and fifty dollars and tickets."

"Even that probably won't be enough," Longarm groused. "Not if this gang is as professional and ruthless as you seem to think they are."

Billy wasn't listening. He drew out his brass pocket watch and consulted it, then said, "If you hurried, you could still catch the afternoon train to Pueblo."

"Are you crazy! It leaves in two hours."

"You could hail a carriage and—"

"Forget it," Longarm snapped. "You really have your gall, Billy. I just got back from Montana, half dead and down twenty pounds, and you drag me in here on my first day off and want to send me off to Cortez in less than two hours. Well, dammit, I won't do it."

"All right. Calm down. You can catch the train tomorrow afternoon. And you can take the rest of the day off and rest, then get a good sleep tonight and be fresh tomorrow morning when you come in for your travel funds and tickets. How does that sound?''

"Like hell," Longarm snapped. "You forgot about the letter promising me a month's paid vacation when I return."

"Well, sure. I guess I can do that."

Longarm came to his feet. The meeting was over. "Billy," he warned, "I want that letter, and if it's not ready tomorrow morning, then I won't be ready to leave for Cortez."

"Custis, why are you acting like you got a big boil on your ass today?"

Longarm just shook his head. "I have to hand it to you, Boss. You've got a real set of brass balls. But that aside, just have the tickets, the money, and the letter ready when I come in tomorrow afternoon."

"You'll also need to see the letter from Miss Mason."

"Okay, add that with the rest."

"I hope that you realize how sensitive this whole business is," Billy said as Longarm headed for the door. "There are lots of important people in Colorado and everywhere else who have become very interested in the history of our Aboriginal Americans."

"Our what?"

"Well, they *were* the first people on the continent," Billy said a little defensively.

"Whatever you say," Longarm replied. "To me, they're Americans first and Indians second. Just like an Irishman or an Italian, say, might think of himself as Irish or Italian, but American first. Savvy?"

"Sure," Billy said, unable to hide his sarcasm. "And I'm glad to see that you are so attuned to the cultural sensitivities in this matter."

"Billy," Longarm said at the door, "you and I have been friends for a good many years, but I have to tell you that you are starting to talk like a gawdamn bureaucrat. And if I were you, I'd be worried."

"Get out of here and get some sleep," Billy ordered. "You're as touchy as a teased polecat and twice as ugly."

Longarm left his boss then. Most days he and Billy could joke around and work well together, but even Billy had his bad days. And he was a pushy bastard at times too. But then, when you went into management and administration, that was what happened to an otherwise fine fella.

Longarm wasted no time clearing out of the Federal Building located near the U.S. Mint on West Colfax Avenue. He was going to head for his rooming house near Cherry Creek and take a long afternoon nap. Then he would go see Miranda and try to smooth things over about the fact that they wouldn't be having much time together until after this job was finished.

Miranda was going to be mad as hell, but what could he do? She'd waited for him before, and he was pretty sure that she'd wait for him now. She'd just have to, dammit. And anyway, he'd have that letter promising him vacation time, and then, with a month off, maybe he'd take her down to New Orleans. He had a few scores to settle there, and then he'd show her the French Quarter and they could have a real, real good time.

Chapter 2

When Longarm arrived at Miranda's place, he was freshly shaven and wearing a clean shirt and pants. And he had a bouquet of red roses clenched in his big fist.

"Hi, honey," he said when she opened her door. "These are for you."

Miranda was a tall, statuesque gal with red hair and green eyes. Longarm thought her beautiful, as did everyone else who had the pleasure of seeing her strolling down the streets of Denver. She had a great, hearty laugh and shared his own slightly bizarre sense of humor.

"My, my!" she exclaimed, giving him a big hug and then dragging him inside. "What an unexpected surprise! Roses! They're beautiful, Custis!"

"They're nothing compared to you," Longarm said, laying the praise on as thick as he could without overdoing it. Miranda had a fiery temper. She was going to go through the ceiling when he finally told her that he was leaving for Cortez tomorrow instead of taking her

11

off on that nice, romantic vacation he'd been promising for the past six months.

"You sure are in a great *vacation* mood this evening," Miranda said. "I've been thinking about what you were saying, whether we should go to California, Mexico, or New Orleans. I've decided that I'd prefer California. Maybe go to San Francisco on the train and see the sights. It'd be nice to see the ocean as well."

"Yeah," Longarm agreed, "it would, but . . ."

"The thing of it is," Miranda said, cutting him off as she found a vase and filled it with water to keep the roses from wilting, "just being together is the important thing. It doesn't matter *where* we are really."

"That's right."

"I've got my boss to give me three weeks off," Miranda was saying, "Two of 'em will be without pay, but I've been saving money for this vacation for a good long while and—"

"Miranda," he said, coming over and placing his hands on her shoulders. "I have some bad news. I have to go out in the field again and I'll be leaving tomorrow."

She spun around and swatted him in the face with the roses.

"Ouch!" Several thorns had stabbed him in the chin.

"How can you do this to me!" Miranda wailed. "This must be the third or fourth time you've left me like this."

Actually, it was the fifth, but Longarm wasn't about to tell Miranda that. "Listen," he said, "I'm getting a signed paper from Billy Vail *promising* me a month's paid vacation when I return from this job."

"But what if you *don't* return!"

"What is that supposed to mean?"

"You could be killed. You've told me about all the close calls you've had over the years. What good is that piece of damned paper going to do if you're shot to death!"

"Settle down, Miranda. I'm not going to get killed. The job they're sending me on this time really doesn't sound at all dangerous. All I have to do is infiltrate a gang of Indian grave robbers and halt the flow of Anasazi artifacts out of this country."

"You're going to Mesa Verde!"

"Among other places. Why?"

"I've been wanting to visit that place for *years*!"

"Now, Miranda," he hedged, realizing where her mind was going, "if you think that I'm going to take you along, then you have another think coming."

"Why?"

"Because the job might have *some* small element of danger and I don't want you to get hurt."

"Then it *is* dangerous! You lied to me!"

Longarm could see that he wasn't getting anywhere and that his hopes for a romantic last evening in Denver were beginning to fade. "Look," he said, "why don't we go out to dinner someplace nice and have fun? We can come back here later and talk about this and—"

"Oh, no! You'll just try to get me to drink too much wine over dinner and then soften me up for a good time in bed." Miranda glared at him. "I know you, Custis!"

And she did, for that was exactly his plan. It was not original, but then again, it was straightforward and uncomplicated, just as he was. "Tell you what," Custis said, "I'll buy you a steak dinner and you can drink water with it if you like."

"Thank you very much!"

"All right, if that doesn't suit you, then drink wine or whiskey!" he exclaimed, getting exasperated. "But this is our last night out for a couple of weeks, and I sure hate the idea of squandering it in a fight. That doesn't do either one of us any good."

"I want to go with you to Mesa Verde. I'll make it fun for you and I'll—"

"No."

"Then I'll stay at Cortez, where I can't possibly be a bother," she told him. "I've done some reading on Mesa Verde, and I know that there are a number of guides that are routinely taking sightseers up there for two-day, three-day, and even week-long trips."

"Miranda, it just won't work."

Her eyes flashed and her chin jutted out stubbornly. "Custis, I'm taking my vacation and it's going to be in Mesa Verde. Maybe you can ignore me, but you can't stop me. It's still a *free* country. You're the law and you ought to know that, for cripes sakes!"

Longarm ground his teeth with frustration. Miranda was a real bulldog when she got an idea in her head. She was as stubborn as a mule, and Longarm knew that the more he tried to talk her out of Mesa Verde, the more determined she'd become.

"All right. We'll leave tomorrow on the afternoon train going south to Pueblo, then take the stage over to Durango and on to Cortez."

"Really!" Her entire demeanor changed from anger to elation. "Custis, do you really mean it!"

"I do. After all, it *is* a free country and you're right saying that I can't stop you."

She fairly danced around the room, light and happy as an elf. "Maybe we could hire a guide together and pose as newlyweds. That way, we'd look like regular tourists and you'd have a perfect cover.''

Longarm blinked with surprise because this was actually a very fine idea. With a woman at his side, he could go on the tour and look like anyone else. And after he'd had the opportunity to poke around in the cliff dwellings and study the layout, then he could leave Miranda with her tour group and strike off on his own after the grave robbers.

''You like the idea, don't you,'' she said, grinning.

''Yeah, actually I do,'' he admitted. ''It's not bad at all.''

''Not bad? It's *brilliant*! But we'll need some props.''

''What do you mean?''

''I mean that, if we are posing as newlyweds, we'll need to buy ourselves a set of *wedding rings*.''

Longarm gulped. He hadn't thought it out, but again, it made sense. It would look funny if they were barefingered. Still, the idea of buying wedding rings made him damned uncomfortable, even queasy in the gut.

''I don't have much money,'' he said, stalling.

''That doesn't matter! We can buy them on credit. I know the man at the jewelry store and he trusts me. Besides, when I tell him that you are a United States deputy marshal with a regular paycheck, he'll—''

''He'll figure that I'm a damn risky customer for credit 'cause I might get ventilated.''

''No, no! Trust me, Custis. He'll give us the credit, and I'm sure that we can find a set of wedding rings that aren't all *that* expensive.''

''But I don't want to get stuck with rings that I don't intend on keeping!''

Miranda's eyes flashed. ''You've told me bunches of

times that the day was coming when you wanted to settle down and be married to me.''

Again, this was true. Another major blunder that was coming back to haunt him.

"You weren't lying to me, were you?" She asked him.

"No, but . . ."

"Then let's go to the jewelry store and get ourselves rings before it closes! Just think what a perfect cover this will be and how much fun we can have playing newlyweds."

To stimulate his imagination, Miranda slipped her arms around his waist and pulled her lovely body tight against his, then nuzzled his neck. Her breath was warm, and when she reached up and nipped his earlobe, Longarm figured that, yes, they would be having a lot of fun together up in Mesa Verde pretending to be tourists with the other folks. So much fun, in fact, that he realized he would need to keep himself on track lest he entirely forget the true purpose of his visit.

"All right. All right," he said, drawing in a deep breath. "Let's get the rings, have some dinner, and then come back and pretend that this is our *wedding* night."

Miranda's green eyes went soft and dreamy. "I'd really like that," she purred. "Will you even carry me over the threshold into this place?"

"Sure," he said, hoping that he didn't pull a muscle in his back. Miranda was a lot of woman. Not fat or sloppy, but tall, heavy-boned, and with plenty of padding in all the right places. She probably weighed close to 150 pounds, and every ounce of it was alive with passion.

They hurried downtown and went into the jewelry store that Miranda had in mind. On the way, she kept

Longarm talking so much that he didn't have time to get nervous or decide to back out of this deal.

"Well, well!" the owner of the jewelry store said when they approached his glass counter filled with rings and other expensive-looking jewelry. "Miranda, it's good to see you again!"

"You too, Mitchell."

"Don't tell me," the impeccably dressed and manicured jeweler said with a sly wink, "you want another wedding ring!"

Longarm's jaw dropped. "What is that supposed—"

"Why, look at that!" Miranda exclaimed, yanking him aside and pointing to a particular jewelry case. "Every one of those rings is beautiful! Mitchell, could you pull out this tray?"

"Why, certainly!"

"Miranda, what did this fella mean when—"

"How much are these!"

"Which ones?" Mitchell asked, smooth and slender fingers caressing the velvet-lined case.

"What about this set," Miranda said, laying her finger on a beautiful diamond ring.

"What taste you have, Miranda!" the jeweler exclaimed. "Better each time, eh?"

He picked up the matching set of wedding and engagement rings. "This set is adorned with a full carat, and I agree that the setting is magnificent! Good choice!"

"Now wait a minute! That looks damned expensive," Longarm said dubiously. "How much?"

"Just six hundred dollars."

Longarm almost buckled at the knees, and managed to shout, "That's a year's wages! Miranda, let's get the hell out of here! I'm not going to put myself forever in hock over diamond rings."

"Wait, wait!" Miranda forced a frozen smile. "Mitchell, why don't you show us a *modest* set of wedding rings. We're a little short of cash."

"She's right about *that*," Longarm said. "I doubt that I have even fifty dollars to my name."

"But I can match that," Miranda said quickly.

The jeweler gave them a very pitying look, then placed the felt display case back under glass. From out of a drawer, he pulled out a cheap case of rings and placed them on the counter. "At this price range I can offer you an engagement and wedding ring set for—"

"Forget the engagement ring," Longarm snapped. "We're at the wedding part now. I want just one ring for her and another for me. And I want them to be cheap."

Mitchell's nose got out of joint, but Longarm didn't care. The jeweler disappeared into the back room. A few minutes later, he emerged with a brown paper bag of rings that he dumped out on the glass counter. These are my cheapest, sir. Some are used, and—"

"Don't matter to me," Longarm said. "Point out the cheapest of the lot and those are the ones that we might buy."

"This pair is only thirty dollars," the jeweler told him in a clipped voice as he stared down at the rings as if they were dirty cockroaches.

"Where's the diamonds!" Miranda cried, squinting down at the cheap-looking rings.

"I'll have to get my jeweler's glass to show you," Mitchell answered.

"Custis, I'm not going to be humiliated by some

crummy little bauble. I want a real diamond, and I expect for you to pay for at least half of it!''

''What about this one?'' Longarm said, pointing to the nicest of the bunch.

Mitchell picked up the ring and looked very unimpressed. Longarm couldn't figure out why because the ring was quite attractive. It had one big diamond surrounded by several small rubies. Longarm thought it perfect, and Miranda must have as well because she said, ''I wouldn't be ashamed to wear this one.''

''How much?'' Longarm asked.

Mitchell rolled his eyes toward heaven. ''I could let you have it for . . . eighty dollars.''

''What about *his* wedding band?'' Miranda asked, holding the ring up to the light and admiring the stones.

''Well, his ring should at least be matching yellow gold. Silver would look very . . . tinny.''

''I agree,'' Miranda said. ''So Custis needs a simple gold wedding band.''

''I can let you have one for another ten dollars. It's very plain and nothing to—''

''That will be fine,'' Longarm said. ''Fit me and let's get this business done with and get out of here before I decide to just forget the whole thing.''

Ten minutes and ninety dollars later, forty-five of which were Longarm's, they marched out of the jewelry store wearing their wedding rings. Half a block down the street, Longarm stopped and said, ''I sure hope he'll buy 'em back when this is over.''

''He will,'' Miranda said before she caught herself.

Longarm looked down at his girlfriend, wondering. But he wisely chose not to say anything, and since they had spent almost all of their cash on rings, they had an inexpensive Mexican dinner with a couple of good bottles of beer. Afterward, they headed back to Miranda's place.

"Don't forget that you promised to carry me over the threshold."

"Aw, come on!"

"We have to get into the spirit of this or it isn't going to work and we won't fool anyone in Mesa Verde! And we might as well start right here and now."

"No," he said, "let's start after we get inside, lock your door, and leap into your bed."

"Carry me, please?"

Longarm picked her up, and immediately revised his estimate of how much Miranda weighed, adding another ten or twenty pounds. Staggering through the door, he caught his toe on a throw rug, and they both crashed to the floor, laughing.

Three or maybe four seconds later, they were tearing off their clothes and racing for the bedroom wearing nothing but their new wedding rings. Longarm pounced on Miranda the way a mountain lion might jump on a deer, and Miranda squealed with delight and wrestled fiercely, pretending to fight him off. They struggled like that for a few minutes, and then he pried her legs apart and entered her with a hard thrust.

"Oh!" Miranda cried. "Please stop!"

She didn't mean it. The woman loved it, and when she locked her legs around his waist, Longarm began to plunge in and out of her like a stallion. He covered her right breast with his mouth and licked her nipple as his body worked. Soon, Miranda was bucking and squealing with pleasure, and then she rolled Longarm over and rode him a while. It wasn't anything like what a couple of newlyweds would probably do in real life, but Longarm didn't give a damn. He and Miranda were great together in bed, and when something worked this well, you didn't screw around and try to change things.

Miranda moved up and down his big rod, her red hair cascading forward over his chest and her breath coming faster and faster. Longarm's fingers were buried into the firm flesh of her buttocks, and he was moving her around and around and groaning with animal pleasure.

"Honey," he grunted, "I'll bet that newlyweds were never this good together!"

"We will be."

Longarm didn't want to know what she meant by that, so he kept quiet and kept her moving over him until her bottom began to twitch and bump. At that moment, Longarm rolled her over and plowed her field good, planting his seed.

In the morning they made love again, only without the pretense and the games. Miranda was feeling very happy. "I am so glad that you decided to let me come with you," she told him.

"You didn't give me any choice."

"That's true," she agreed. "But at least you're not acting grumpy or trying to punish me for my insistence. I like a man who can lose gracefully."

Longarm didn't like her use of the word "lose," but he managed not to make an issue of it. He left Miranda and went over to the Federal Building, where he found that his travel money and his letter from Billy guaranteeing him a month's paid vacation were waiting.

"There are also tickets in that manila envelope," Billy told him.

"Coach, no doubt."

"Of course! What did you expect, first class?"

21

"Yeah, that would have been nice."

"Not on the taxpayers' money," Billy said. "Anyway, here is the letter from Miss Mason. Please give her my best regards and try not to seduce her. She's an old family friend."

"Sure, sure," Longarm said, having already decided that it was not in his own best interests to mention that Miranda was coming along to keep him company. "Anything else?"

"Not that I can think of," Billy said. "Oh, yeah, I do have a few newspaper articles on murders that I suspect might be related to his Anasazi artifact gang."

Billy went to his desk and rummaged around among its clutter until he found an envelope. "Read these accounts. In every one it mentions that the victim was in some way, shape, or form connected to Anasazi artifacts."

Longarm noticed the envelope's thickness.

"There's that many people involved?"

"And more every year," Billy assured him. "Scientists are describing Mesa Verde, Hovenweep, and some of the other ruins that are scattered all over the Four Corners area as the greatest archaeological sites in America."

"I see."

"Do this job well," Billy said, "and there might be a promotion in store for you this fall."

"Like you got to a desk job? No, thanks!"

Billy wasn't offended. Quite the contrary. He just smiled, and then he went back to his desk as Longarm headed for the train depot to get Miranda a ticket to Pueblo. She wouldn't be all that pleased riding coach either, but their destination was less than a full day's

journey away, and they could easily tolerate the sometimes rough and ready men who frequented the third-
class coach cars and who could be a bit uncouth and
insulting.

Chapter 3

Longarm and Miranda were a little late getting to the train station, and damned if the third-class coach wasn't nearly filled with a collection of rough cowboys, miners, and workingmen headed south. Miranda was the only young woman to enter this coach, and although Longarm was not a jealous man, he bristled at the bold and hungry-eyed looks she received as they moved down the aisle searching for a pair of seats together.

Unfortunately, there weren't any. In fact, there was only *one* empty seat in the entire coach, and the only reason it was empty was that it rested beside one of the biggest, dirtiest-looking men Longarm had seen in a good while. He must have been a mountain man or a trapper because he was wearing buckskins and a thick black beard. A huge Bowie knife protruded from under a beaded Indian belt. The man stank like a dead animal.

"Oh, the hell with this," Longarm snapped. "We'll go find the conductor and change our tickets to first class."

"What's the matter?" the mountain man challenged,

eyes fixed on Miranda's ample bosom. "I don't mind the lady sitting here beside me. Maybe we could have ourselves a little fun, huh, lady?"

"I'd rather sit beside a goat," Miranda replied.

The mountain man's eyes blazed with sudden anger. "Well, ain't you the real uppity little bitch. You ain't so gawdamn grand! I've fucked prettier than you more'n once."

Longarm slapped the mountain man across the face so hard his lips broke and bled. "Mister, apologize to the lady or prepare to learn some manners."

The mountain man wiped a big paw across his mouth, saw the blood, and exploded. "You sonofabitch, nobody slaps Abe Tasker and lives to tell about it! I'll gut you like a fat buck!"

Longarm would have sledged Tasker in the face and maybe ended the fight quick, except that someone pushed Miranda in between them, and by the time he shoved her clear, the mountain man was out of his seat and on his feet with that giant Bowie knife clenched in his fist.

Longarm drew his six-gun and said, "Drop the knife or I'll drop you in your tracks!"

"No, you won't," Tasker said, grabbing Miranda and holding her in front of him as a shield. He placed his knife to Miranda's throat and laughed meanly. "Drop the gun or I'll slit her pretty gullet."

Longarm felt a sudden rivulet of sweat run down his spine. Tasker was clearly a lunatic. He looked as if he might even enjoy killing Miranda.

"All right," Longarm said, dropping his double-action Colt .44-.40 to the floor. "Just turn her loose and we can settle this with our fists."

Tasker giggled obscenely, then pushed Miranda aside.

26

"Sorry," he said, waving the Bowie back and forth, "but I'd rather fight with knives."

"I don't have anything but a pocket knife," Longarm said tightly.

"Too bad," the mountain man replied, taking a vicious swipe at Longarm's belly and barely missing.

Longarm had had all of this he was going to take. Any minute, some fool might decide to try to help him and get himself skewered. The lawman reached for his watch. Its chain, instead of being attached to a watch fob, was affixed to a very mean-looking twin-barreled .44-caliber derringer.

"Your turn," Longarm said, cocking the derringer. "Drop the knife or I'll put two bullets through your brisket. And I can't miss at this range."

Tasker squinted at the derringer. It was compact, but the double muzzles were plenty big and intimidating. Tasker dropped his Bowie knife and raised his big fists. "You said something about fighting?"

"Custis," Miranda said, "why don't you do the whole world a favor and just shoot him? Sure would be the easiest and best thing to do."

"Shut up, woman!"

In reply, Miranda kicked Tasker in the shin so hard that the mountain man let out a yip of pain. Longarm believed in taking advantage of opportunities, so he punched the man right between the eyes and dropped him in the aisle.

"Miranda, why don't you take the man's seat," he said, "while I escort him off the train since he is unfit to be among civilized company."

But Tasker wasn't ready to be "escorted" anywhere. He crawled to his feet, ducked a punch, and charged into Longarm, grabbing him in a crushing bear hug.

27

They fell, but now Tasker was on top, and Longarm took one of his thundering punches, and realized that he might lose consciousness if he took another. Still, he was pinned in the aisle with no room to maneuver. He couldn't get any leverage in his punch, so he jammed his derringer sideways between their bodies and pulled the trigger.

The explosion was muffled, and the bullet ripped into the floor under a nearby seat just as Longarm had intended. It also burned their flesh, but it made Tasker rear back, and that was all that Longarm needed to break free and unleash a jolting overhand right that landed on Tasker's nose and broke it with a crunching sound. Longarm jumped up and swarmed all over the man, landing heavy punches that beat him to the floor. When Tasker stopped trying to fight back and his eyes rolled up into his forehead, Longarm grabbed him and dragged him up the aisle, and then out of the coach and onto the open platform between the swaying coaches.

"You got *two* choices!" Longarm yelled. "You can either stay right here until this train reaches Pueblo, or you can take a flying leap into the brush and walk to Pueblo!"

Tasker's eyes widened. "Don't pitch me over the side! Gawdammit, as fast as this train is goin', I could break my neck in the fall!"

Longarm stepped away. Tasker was a mess. One of his eyes was swollen almost shut, and his nose ran with blood. "Tasker, when this train reaches Pueblo, you better not let me see you even for a minute! Do you understand!"

The mountain man's eyes blazed with hatred. "You can't get away with doin' this to me! I bought a ticket just the same as you and that woman!"

"Yeah, well, I'll have to talk to the railroad about their policy of letting *animals* have seats," Longarm gritted out.

He pivoted and started to go back into the coach, but Tasker reached out, grabbed him by the ankle, and tripped him. Then, the big man was on him again, and they were rolling and wrestling around on the platform.

Tasker was bull-strong, and Longarm was not in his best fighting condition. As they each struggled for advantage, Longarm had the impression that he was going to lose, and so, with Tasker's big hands inching toward his throat, he sledged two hard punches into Tasker's already broken nose.

The mountain man hollered, and his grip loosened just enough for Longarm to squirm free and hit him in the side of the jaw, dislocating or maybe even breaking it. Longarm grabbed the man by the back of his leather shirt and his britches and heaved him off the train, hearing the man's cry end abruptly as he struck the roadbed and then rolled end over end down into a ditch. The man crawled to his knees, then collapsed. Longarm had no energy left to waste on pity, and so he waved Tasker good-bye and good riddance.

Miranda hurried out and hugged him tightly. "I was afraid that *you* were going to be killed or thrown off the train."

"So was I."

"Custis, I sure didn't think that you could whip someone *that* big."

Longarm flexed his battered hands. "There's a prizefighter who says that the bigger they are the harder they fall. That huge sonofabitch fell pretty hard."

"Are you all right?"

"My ribs hurt and one side of my face is numb and

29

probably swelling up like a melon. Other than that and a few scraped knuckles, I'm okay."

"Well," Miranda said, "at least now we'll be able to sit together all the rest of the way down to Pueblo."

"Yeah," he said, "but if we tell people that we are newlyweds, they're just naturally going to think that you've already been beating up on me."

"Fat chance of that," Miranda scoffed, helping him back into the coach. No one challenged him with their eyes or stared at Miranda the way they had earlier.

The rest of the trip down to Pueblo was blessedly uneventful. Longarm accepted a couple of drinks from sympathetic passengers, and the whiskey made him feel almost human. Still, he was more than a little unhappy with the way that this trip was starting. Miranda was supposed to make things *easier,* not harder. If she hadn't been along, he wouldn't have felt compelled to defend her honor and fight Tasker. It might have been an uneventful trip and he'd be feeling a whole lot better than he was feeling now.

Oh, well. Miranda was with him, and she wasn't going to be sent back home or turned away now. The woman had her heart set on seeing those Mesa Verde ruins, and she would be awful nice to have around starting tonight in Pueblo. It would feel mighty good when she bound his tender ribs, soaked his battered knuckles and swelling eye. She could tend to his battle wounds, and that was far better than having to tend to himself.

Longarm liked Pueblo, and had passed through it whenever he had assignments to the south. The town had been founded by the famed mountain man and trader Jim Beckwourth in 1842, at the confluence of Fountain Creek and the Arkansas River. Located near plenty of good grass and water, the town grew quickly, and soon became a major trading settlement. On the dusty streets of Pueblo you could see Indians, Mexicans, cowboys, railroad workers, and miners. With the railroad's arrival in 1872, ranching and farming had boomed, and valuable minerals had been found just to the west of town. Now, there were smelters and foundries employing hundreds of workmen.

"I didn't realize that it was so big," Miranda said after they disembarked from the train and started toward what Longarm knew was a respectable hotel.

"Pueblo is a fine place to live and raise a family," Longarm said. "Miners are bringing in their families, and women always change the look and feel of a town. There are a few less saloons, a few more churches than there were just a year ago."

"And you don't approve of that?" Miranda asked, looking up at him.

"No, that's fine with me," Longarm said. "We used to have a lot of trouble here, but they hired a good marshal and he's got two outstanding deputies."

"How long will we be here?"

"Two nights," Longarm told her. "Monday morning we'll catch a stage west to Durango. That will take a few days' hard travel over the southern Rockies."

"I *love* travel and adventure," Miranda said. "Especially with you."

"I like traveling, but but sometimes it gets boring. I expect that after seeing some of the roads we're going to be carried over, you'll have had your fill of stagecoach travel by the time we reach Durango. It's a hard trip, but the country is pretty."

"You won't hear me complain," she assured him.

"Wouldn't do you any good. With any luck, we'll

31

have the coach to ourselves, but don't count on it."

"I don't care, as long as Tasker doesn't show up and expect to ride along. Whew! I never knew a human being could smell so bad. He must not have taken a bath since he was a baby."

Longarm chuckled. "I suspect that might be true. And sometimes, you get lucky and meet very nice people on these stagecoaches. It's all the luck of the draw."

"Yes, I'm sure that it is. Just remember that we're supposed to be *married*."

Longarm stopped outside the Belmont Hotel and winked down at Miranda. "Why don't you set about reminding me of that when we get up to our room?"

"You didn't get as beat up as I thought," Miranda said, taking his arm as they went inside.

"Marshal Long!" an older woman, wearing a pink shawl and with her silver hair pinned up around her pleasant face, cried. "It's good to see you again!"

"Well, thank you, Mrs. Jackson," he said. "And allow me to introduce my wife Miranda."

"Congratulations!" She gave Miranda a big hug.

"Thank you," Miranda said. "We're on our honeymoon and heading for Mesa Verde."

"Why go there when you can stay here?" the older woman asked. "I shouldn't think you'd want to waste so much time riding in a stagecoach when you could be . . . enjoying yourselves right here in beautiful Pueblo."

"Miranda has always wanted to see the Anasazi cliff dwellings," Longarm explained.

"Just a bunch of old caves and buildings, or at least so I'm told," Mrs. Jackson said. "Indian stuff, and spooky at that. We have two excellent museums right here in town, and you can see all the old bones, pots, and baskets right here."

"I'd still like to see Mesa Verde," Miranda said. "But I'm sure that we'll enjoy our stay here. The train ride down was a little more eventful than expected."

Mrs. Jackson clucked her tongue and put her hands on her skinny hips. "Who hit you, Custis? Wasn't her, was it?"

"No," he said with a silly grin. "But I'd appreciate a good bath and some Epsom salts. We had some trouble with a man who needed a lesson in civility and manners."

"I hope he looks worse than you do," Mrs. Jackson said.

"I expect that he does," Longarm agreed. "I broke both his nose and his jaw, and he was already ugly."

Mrs. Jackson laughed and said, "I'll give you my best room for the same price I always charge you for a single. Ain't exactly what anyone would call a 'honeymoon suite,' but it has pretty wallpaper and nicer furniture than you're used to. Some of it was my grandmother's, and I want you to be careful and not bust up the bed."

Miranda blushed, but Longarm pretended not to notice as they followed the woman up the stairs to the second floor and then down to Room 214. The room was nice, with some beautiful old furniture and a real brass bed with a lace-covered canopy and real oil paintings on the walls.

"Hazel, this is perfect," Longarm said to Mrs. Jackson.

"It really is," Miranda agreed.

"I thought you'd be pleased," the woman replied. "Now, I'll have that bath and salts brought up at once along with a bottle of free champagne."

"Hazel, you've a generous and romantic heart," Longarm told her.

"Your bride is very pretty, Custis. Can't imagine why she would have married a big ugly galoot like you. But I guess that's her secret."

Longarm liked to be teased, and he was smiling when Mrs. Jackson closed the door behind them.

"She really likes you," Miranda said.

"The feeling is mutual." Longarm kissed Miranda and they sat down on the bed, her head resting on his shoulder, both very content to wait for the bath and the champagne.

Chapter 4

"The stagecoach for Durango and Cortez always leaves at noon on Monday and Friday," Longarm explained as he and Miranda enjoyed breakfast at a nearby cafe. "It comes in from Durango and stays only long enough to change horses and drivers, then turns around and heads back again."

"Well, this is definitely Monday," Miranda said, glancing over at a wall clock, "and we've got all morning to enjoy ourselves."

Longarm yawned. "I wish we'd have slept a few more hours. We stayed up kind of late."

"Well," Miranda whispered across the table, "that's because we made love *three* times. No wonder we're both tired this morning. I'm even a little sore!"

Longarm stifled a smile. They *had* overindulged a bit last evening. "It must have been because we were in the honeymoon suite."

Longarm finished his coffee, and resisted the urge to smoke one of his cigarillos because they were pretty smelly. So he just leaned back and waited until Miranda finished her own breakfast. Miranda was a slow eater. She was relaxed at almost everything except lovemaking, and then she turned into a spitfire.

"You look good to me this morning," he said as she finished her toast.

"Does that mean that you want to go back to the hotel room and do it *again*?"

"Yeah, but I think we'd better go over to the stagecoach office after we leave here and buy our tickets. I just don't want to run any risk of the coach being sold out. That isn't very likely, but it never hurts to get your tickets before the last minute."

"All right," Miranda said, delicately wiping away a milk mustache. "Let's go."

Longarm paid the tab, and they headed up the street toward the stage station. When they arrived, it was deserted except for the stage-line owner, Bill Fieldman, an ex-cowpoke who had been thrown by way too many broncs and who walked with a pronounced limp.

"Well, howdy, Marshal Long," Bill said, forking some oat hay into a corral full of stout horses. "Real good to see you again."

"Nice to see you too, Bill. This is my wife Miranda."

Bill grinned from ear to ear. He was a trim, muscular man in his fifties with a lined and weathered face. "My pleasure, ma'am!"

"How's business?" Longarm asked.

"To be honest, it's damn poor since last month when our stagecoach was robbed along with all the passengers."

"Is that right?"

"Why, sure. I thought you feds might even have heard the news up in Denver, but I guess not."

"No," Longarm told him. "What happened?"

36

"There's a gang of thieves operating in this neck of the country. They've robbed us three times in the last three months, and they've robbed some other travelers as well."

"How many are in the gang?"

"Four, and sometimes even five," Bill said. "They wear bandannas, of course, so no one knows who they are. They hide along the road and then get the drop on our guard and driver real sudden-like. After that, they order 'em to hand over all their valuables or get shot."

"Has anyone been killed yet?"

"Last time they robbed my stage, they shot my guard. Didn't kill him, but he'll never have the use of his left arm again. I can't get a replacement because everyone is so scared."

"What about drivers?"

"I've got old Jessie driving the stage over from Durango that's supposed to arrive today," Bill said. "He ain't afraid of no one, but I'm damned worried that he might get mad and pull a gun and get hisself shot."

"Is there a stage going back to Durango today?"

"I think so. I've got a driver—but no shotgun, even though I've offered to pay double wages."

"Who is the westbound driver?"

"A fella named Charley Blue. He's another crusty old fella that's been driving stages for too many years to know anything better. Charley is one hell of a reinsman, but he's cantankerous and he says that he don't need no shotgun guard."

"How many passengers are on this trip west?"

"Well," Bill drawled, looking pained, "that's what I mean about business being so poor. I only got one other couple willing to ride the coach over to Durango. He's a newspaperman just hired fresh out of college and his

37

wife is a new schoolteacher. Both are going to jobs in Durango. If it weren't for that, I doubt that they'd be so anxious to go over the mountains.''

Longarm turned and looked at Miranda. "It might be better if you stayed here. There's no telling what could happen if this gang decides to hit again.''

"I'm *going*," Miranda said, leaving little room for argument. "And I can handle a gun if necessary. Just give me one and I'll show you.''

Longarm led her out behind the station, and then he handed her his pistol. Bill was with them when Miranda said, "Point me out a target.''

"The barn door," Longarm said in jest.

"No," Miranda said, "how about that rusty tin can resting just to the right of the door?''

"You're going to try and hit that?'' Bill asked, looking very skeptical.

"I am," Miranda said, using a two-handed grip on Longarm's pistol and taking careful aim. The Colt bucked, and a couple of chickens nearby erupted into squawking flight, but damned if the tin can didn't skip high up into the air and strike the barn door.

"Well, I'll be jingoed!'' Bill said with amazement. "Of all the luck, she really hit the damned thing!''

"Luck, my ruffled tail feathers," Miranda said, waiting until the can came to rest and then taking quick aim and neatly drilling it a second time.

Longarm clucked his tongue with admiration. "You never told me you could shoot like that!''

"You never asked, and I didn't see any point in bringing it up," Miranda replied, handing Custis his revolver back. "But I learned when I was a girl living on the Kansas prairie in a soddie. My father expected me to bring one rabbit or large bird home for each bullet he gave me. I'll admit to missing sometimes, but not very often, because we were poor and ammunition was expensive."

"If she wasn't a woman," Bill said, "I'd hire *her* to be the guard."

"I'll be the guard," Longarm said. "Miranda, can you handle a rifle?"

"You bet I can."

"Bill, why don't you put a rifle and pistol in the coach for Miranda? We'll both ride inside, and if that gang decides to hold up the stage, we'll give them one hell of an unpleasant surprise."

"You sure?" Bill asked. "You could both get shot."

"That's right, but this might be the only way to rid the territory of that gang. I can drop two of them before they know what hit them. Miranda can shoot at least one, and the fight will be over in a hurry."

"I dunno," Bill said, looking extremely worried. "It's one thing to hire a man and pay him for risking his damned neck, but asking a woman to do it, well . . ."

"Give us free tickets to Cortez," Miranda said. "I think that would be payment enough, don't you, Custis?"

"Sure," Longarm agreed. "We'll do it for a free ride and eats to Cortez. How does that square with you, Bill?"

"It sits just fine," the older man said. "And I'm sure that Charley will be happy too. He's tough, but he's no match for a gang of highwaymen."

Longarm consulted his pocket watch. "We'll be going back to the Belmont to wait until it's time to leave."

"I'll send a boy over to fetch you," Bill said. "I sure appreciate this. I've got mail and supplies that need to go west, and I was trying to decide whether or not to take the chance of sending them. Now I sure will."

"Good," Longarm said, taking Miranda's arm and steering her back toward their hotel.

"Sure sorry that you have to leave," Mrs. Jackson said when they returned. "There's good fishing down at the creek and the wild berries are waiting to be picked. I got a basketful yesterday, and I'm going to make a pie tonight that I'd like you to enjoy."

"We'd like that," Longarm said, meaning it, "but we are taking today's stage."

"I expected you would change your mind after hearing about the robberies," she said. "Might be better to come see Mesa Verde next year when its safer."

"You know that I'm a lawman. I can't and won't run from trouble."

"What about your pretty wife?" the old lady asked with disapproval. "She'd sure be a prize for them outlaws."

"I'll be fine," Miranda assured her.

"I sure hope so! A woman as pretty as you are has no business taking a stagecoach over them mountains when outlaws are raising Cain with the common folks."

"Please don't worry," Miranda said.

"Don't make sense to me to risk your neck to see some Indian bones and pots. Not when we got them right here in our own museums. That's my opinion."

Longarm managed to escape the woman and take Miranda up to their hotel room. They jumped into bed and made love again, and then napped for a couple of hours before a boy came to knock on their door.

"Stagecoach just got here!" the boy called. "Bill says to come on over 'cause Charley don't wait for nobody."

"We'll be along directly," Longarm said, piling out of bed and dressing quickly.

It took Miranda a few more minutes, and then they gathered their bags and headed downstairs.

"Damned foolishness!" Mrs. Jackson called as they waved her good-bye and hurried outside. "You take care of that pretty girl now!"

"I will," Longarm shouted back at the hotel owner. "Don't you worry about that!"

When they arrived at the stage station, Bill introduced them to Charley Blue. He was bearded and of average height, in his late fifties, with sloping shoulders and muscular arms. He was also a tobacco chewer, and kept spitting into the dust.

"I sure don't approve of a guard who brings along a woman," Charley grumped. "Damned if it makes any sense at all to me, Marshal Long."

"Miranda is a good shot, and I'll be riding down in the coach with her. Where are the other passengers that are supposed to be going to Durango?"

"Here they come now," Bill said, pointing up the street at a handsome young couple. The husband was dressed in a dark suit, and his young wife wore a flowered dress. Both were lugging heavy suitcases, and looked tired and under a great deal of strain. Longarm would have bet anything they'd spent a lot of time arguing about the wisdom of taking this journey, even though they could risk losing their Durango jobs.

The young man's name was Trent Roe, and his wife was named Esther. Longarm took Roe's measure, and saw that the young man looked determined but would probably not be much help in a gunfight. His wife was slender and delicate-looking, her black hair mussed.

"All aboard," Charley called after the introductions. "We got a long way to go before we reach the overnight station."

Longarm helped Miranda into the stagecoach, and Trent did the same for Esther. They settled in comfortably enough and smiled at each other as Bill shoved both a Winchester and a shotgun into the coach, saying, "I hope you don't need these, but you might. Good luck."

"Thanks," Longarm answered.

"Yeah, thanks," Roe said, trying to compose himself.

The stage lurched quite suddenly, almost spilling the Roe couple into the leg space between the seats. Looking awkward and embarrassed, they climbed back onto their rear-facing seats.

"We've never ridden in a stagecoach," Roe said, explaining the obvious. "We're from the East."

"Where exactly?" Longarm asked.

"Columbus, Ohio," Esther answered. "We met at college and discovered that we both had always dreamed of living in the American West."

"How do you like it so far?" Miranda asked.

"We like it a lot," Trent said. "We loved both Cheyenne and Denver, but we've heard that Durango is even nicer."

"It's a beautiful town," Longarm agreed. "You won't be disappointed."

"Are the winters real bad?" Esther asked.

"Oh," Longarm answered, "not that bad. Probably not as severe as you had in Ohio."

The four of them talked all afternoon as the stage rolled upward into the foothills of the Rockies, and it was enjoyable. Longarm felt guilty having to lie to the Roes about him and Miranda being married, but there was no help for it.

"I can't believe that we're actually riding in the same coach with a Western marshal," Esther gushed. "I've seen the dime novels with all the shooting and Indians and . . . well, have you ever had to use that gun you wear?''

"Plenty of times," Longarm said without elaboration. "But I'm hoping that it won't come in handy this trip."

"So are we," Trent added fervently. "I have a gun in my pocket, but I've never shot it before."

"Maybe I'd better take a look at it. Just to make sure that it is safe to use."

The young journalist dragged an old Navy Colt out of his pocket. It was a percussion pistol, and loaded with black powder and ball but no percussion caps, rendering it useless.

"What about the caps?" Longarm asked.

"The man who sold it to me said that I shouldn't put them on unless I really have to. Do you agree, Marshal?"

"No, I don't. Putting caps on takes a few seconds that could very well mean the difference between life and death. Do you have any?"

"In my suitcase tied to the back of the stagecoach," Trent said sheepishly.

"Well, the first time we stop, let's cap this thing and make sure that it shoots straight," Longarm said, handing the old weapon back to the reporter. "You really need to get familiar with a gun *before* you need it. That way, there are no unpleasant surprises."

"I'm sure he's right, darling," the schoolteacher said. She smiled at Longarm. "We feel a *lot* safer with you aboard, Marshal. I shouldn't admit this, and I know that it will embarrass my husband, but we almost backed out of this trip and returned to Denver to look for other jobs. Your presence made the difference between going forward . . . or going back."

"Well," Longarm said, a little humbled by that admission and the responsibility that it implied, "chances are that we'll have no trouble, but at least we'll be ready if it comes."

"Yeah," Trent fretted. "I sure hope those caps didn't fall out of my bags."

"Me too," Longarm said, looking at Miranda, who winked back at him.

That evening, just as the sun was setting and right after their supper, Longarm and young Trent walked out from the stage stop where they would spend the night and tested the old Navy Colt. Trent had found the caps, and they fired and reloaded the cylinder several times, Longarm giving the Easterner some professional tips on how to aim and slowly squeeze the trigger.

"I can't believe how good a shot you are," Trent said after Longarm drew his own gun and obliterated several small targets to demonstrate the proper technique.

"I've been shooting since I was knee high to a ground squirrel," Longarm confessed. "I can't remember when I wasn't out hunting and shooting. But you don't have to start early in life. Mostly, you just have to remember not to get rattled and take your time aiming and firing."

"But I'd be dead if I had to defend myself against someone like you."

"Yeah, you would," Longarm agreed, realizing it was silly to argue that point. "But the thing of it is, most gunfights take place in saloons between a couple of drunks who can hardly stand up, let alone take aim and hit a target."

"I'm not much of a drinker and I doubt I'll ever go to a saloon."

"Oh, sure you will," Longarm told him. "Western saloons are like its people. Some are good and some are very bad. There's both kinds in Durango, and there's nothing wrong with a man having a glass of whiskey or beer once in a while with his friends. Just make sure that you know which places are safe and which are not.''

"How do I do that?''

"You make the right friends in town and they'll tell you,'' Longarm explained.

"You think we're going to have trouble with that gang?''

"I honestly don't know.''

"Do you *want* them to try and rob us so that you can kill or arrest them?''

"No,'' Longarm said, realizing that he did not. "If I were alone or with other experienced lawmen, sure. But with you, Miranda, and your pretty young wife, I'd be mostly worried about one of you getting shot.''

"If we do get attacked, they won't get much of value from Esther and me. I'll bet that everything we own together isn't worth but ten or fifteen dollars.''

"You'll do well in Durango,'' Longarm told them. "Both of you working and all.''

"You know anything about the *Durango Daily* newspaper that I'm to work for?''

"No.''

"I was lucky to get a job in the same town as Esther. Real lucky.''

"Maybe the lucky ones are the people that were fortunate enough to hire a pair like you,'' Longarm said. "That's the way that I'd look at it.''

"Thanks. And I want you to know that, if we're attacked, I won't do anything cowardly or stupid. I'll do exactly what you say, Marshal. I'm well aware that this is *your* field of expertise, not mine.''

"Glad to hear that you understand that,'' Longarm told the earnest young man. "And stop worrying so much and enjoy the scenery, which will be pretty spectacular tomorrow.''

"We will." Trent excused himself and went into the big log cabin that combined passenger sleeping quarters with a kitchen.

Longarm lingered outside, enjoying the scent of pines and the first stars of the evening. Soon Miranda came out to join him, and she took his hand in her own and said, "A penny for your thoughts."

"I was just wishing on a star that we don't get hit by that gang. Not with you and that young couple on board."

"What will happen will happen and it will all work out for the best," Miranda told him. "I don't feel a bit afraid. Not with you beside me."

Longarm inhaled a deep lungful of the clean mountain air. He was flattered, but still worried.

Chapter 5

They left the stage station at dawn when the air was crisp and there was a thin layer of ice on the water trough. The new team of horses was feeling frisky in the frosty morning air, and they were a handful to harness. All four animals wanted to run as soon as they left the station, and Charley let them, so that his passengers were hanging on for their lives as they shot through the pines and up the narrow, winding road heading southwest. All that day they struggled up the eastern slope of the Sangre de Cristo Mountains, and the day after that rolled down into a lush cattle-ranching paradise where some of the biggest ranches in Colorado were to be found.

The Roes were in awe of this Colorado high country, and Longarm could see that Miranda was equally impressed by the high mountain forests, rugged peaks, and vast pine-ringed valleys. Sometimes, Longarm and Trent Roe took turns riding shotgun on top, where the pine-scented air was a tonic. It was during one of those times that Longarm quizzed Charley Blue about the stagecoach gang, hoping to learn everything he could in order to be as well prepared as possible.

"Marshal, I've never been driving when this stage has been attacked and robbed. However, I expect that my luck . . . or theirs . . . is about ready to run out. If those murderin' jaspers get within range of my rifle, they'll wish they'd have stayed away!"

Charley's rifle was nothing but an old single-shot Civil War antique that had seen far better days. There was, however, no doubting Charley's sincere belief that he could whittle down the odds in a big hurry.

"It appears to me that you have been driving these coaches for a lot of years," Longarm remarked, noting how skillfully the driver handled this high-spirited team.

"Yeah, I went to California back in 1851 to get rich in them cold Sierra rivers, but got pneumonia instead. I almost died, and probably would have if an Indian gal hadn't taken pity on my old hide and nursed me back to health. She was a Pomo Indian. I married her, but she died a few years later, and that like to broke my heart. Mik-ta was the finest woman God ever made. I started drivin' coaches back and forth between Sacramento and the gold fields. Was a friend of John Sutter too! But then he got ruined."

"I understand that Sutter was once considered to be the richest man in California."

"Oh, he was! John Augustus Sutter owned thousands of cattle, sheep, and horses. Had hundreds of Indians workin' his orchards and fields. He was the biggest-hearted man that I ever knew, and that was part of his problem. He gave too much away! Why, he even sent supplies and men up to help rescue some of them poor folks in the Donner Party."

"Is that a fact?"

"Yep. Sutter was a good man, but his downfall began the day that he and John Marshal discovered gold beside their new sawmill on the American River. After that, everything he touched turned to dust. The Forty-Niners swarmed over his lands like famished locusts, and they cleaned him out. All his hired help ran off to get rich in the rivers, and Sutter had no one to help him protect his property. And then too, I hate to say it, but the man was a slave to drink."

"When did you leave the California gold fields and come to Colorado?"

"I arrived in 1858 with about fifty thousand other miners stampeding to the Pikes Peak gold rush. Went to Central City and worked in the mines for a couple of years. When I wasn't down in a mine, I panned the streams, but I spent my gold dust faster'n I could pan it. Prices went crazy. You never seen such a bad collection of thieves as was in Central City! And there were the usual cold-hearted whores, gamblers, pickpockets, and cutthroats. Worst bunch of scum that ever collected anywhere on Earth, and I was right smack in the middle of 'em all. Got fed up with it and got tired of eatin' irregular."

"Mining is a hard life," Longarm agreed.

"It's a man-killer."

"So what did you do next?"

"Got me a job as a mule skinner driving ore wagons, but I just hated them stubborn bastards."

"They can be ornery."

"Oh, hell, yes, they can! Now a horse, they can be mean, but they're not smart so they don't get the drop on you very often. But an ornery mule will plot his revenge over some little thing you might have done like tanning his backside. He'll wait and wait and then, when you're least expecting it, he'll nail you to the barn door with his hooves or his teeth! One did that to me and I shot the sneaky bastard. Blasted a hole in his ass!''

Longarm could not help but grin. ''Did you kill him?''

''No,'' Charley said, looking pained, ''but for the rest of his years he walked with a hitch in his giddy-up! I would have killed him for sure, but his owner bashed me across the back of the head with a two-by-four. I was knocked out cold for two hours. When I woke up, I was fired, of course.''

''Of course,'' Longarm said. ''Well, you are a top-notch driver of a stagecoach team.''

''Thank you! I hope that you can use a gun and a rifle as well as I can drive. We just might need to fight our way into Durango.''

''Where is this gang in the habit of striking?''

''Oh, they got so much country to do it in that they're impossible to predict. The only good thing about it is that they're decent enough to give us warning instead of just blowing us off the top of this coach.''

''That's what I was told.''

''You've probably killed a lot of men before, haven't you, Marshal?''

''Yes, but I take no satisfaction in it. Every man that I've ever killed left me no choice. I try to *arrest* outlaws, not execute them.''

''Try to execute this bunch,'' Charley suggested. '' 'Cause they're just begging for it. The shotgun guard they shot was a friend of mine. Crippled for life, and with a pretty little gal at home and two small children.''

''Did you ever marry, Charley?''

''Just that Pomo girl. Ever since then, I've been

chasin' rainbows and gold nuggets, and I still pan every chance that I get. Wherever there is a clear stream or a river nearby, you'll find me with my gold pan. Someday, I'm going to find a nugget about the size of a goose egg and that'll be my retirement. I'll buy a little house in Durango and marry a sweet widow woman to feed and keep me warm in the winter. I already got my eye on a feisty old gal. She ain't much on looks, but the truth of it is that I'm no prize either.''

"That sounds like a good idea."

"Marshal," Charley said, "you sure married a looker! Whoo-wee! She is *beautiful*!"

Longarm was flattered, even though he wasn't really married. "You think Miranda is a catch, huh?"

"Hell, yes! Why, if I were young again and she was on the loose, I'd be howling like a Kentucky hound dog in the moonlight and then barkin' up her tree!"

Longarm had a good belly laugh over that. "Well," he finally said, "I have to admit that Miranda is quite a girl."

"You're on your honeymoon, or so I've heard."

"That's about the size of it," Longarm said, "but I'd appreciate it if you didn't tell anyone that I was a federal officer. I've already asked the Roes not to mention the fact. I know a couple of folks in Durango, but not many. I know almost no one in Cortez."

"So," Charley said, "if I read you right, this trip is more than just a honeymoon?"

"That's right."

"Bet the government sent you down here and on this coach just to capture this outlaw gang! Ain't that the truth?"

"You're as sharp as they come, Charley."

The old driver chuckled. "Yeah, I'm a lot smarter

than I appear. Why, if I'd used my brains instead of my poor aching back, I might have amounted to something more than run-down stage driver.''

"You seem to like your job.''

"Oh, I do! I like it aplenty, but I don't want to get shot to death.''

"Don't worry,'' Longarm said. "As long as this bunch doesn't shoot first and ask questions later, we'll be fine. Just don't fly off the handle and start blazing away with that hogleg on your hip or that old rifle.''

"You're telling me to let you take the lead if there is trouble.''

"That's right. With the women and the greenhorn down below, I want to reach Durango without any trouble, but I'm prepared if it comes.''

"I saw you showin' the kid how to shoot last night after supper. He gonna be any help if we need him?''

"I think so,'' Longarm answered. "Trent doesn't know much, but he strikes me as having pluck.''

"He'd better have pluck if he plans to be a newspaperman. It's not uncommon for reporters to get shot for what they write about in this part of the country. Why do you think there is a job in Durango?''

"I dunno,'' Longarm replied. "I figured that someone moved on, or the paper is expanding, or something like that.''

"Nope. The last reporter was ambushed one night.''

"Did they catch his murderer?''

"Nope. The thing of it was, the reporter had written so many bad things about so many of the town folks that there were too many suspects to narrow it down to any one person. People are tetchy out here. You write about them in a bad light, they'd just as soon as shoot you in the gizzard as spit in your eye.''

"I'd better have a talk about that with Trent," Long-arm said with a frown. "I don't want him to make the same mistake as his predecessor."

"His who?"

"The reporter who was killed."

"Oh, yeah. Well, my advice would be to give that young greenhorn all the shooting lessons you can before we get to Durango and then trust that the Good Lord will give him enough wisdom not to insult the wrong people."

That evening they stopped at a high mountain lodge, where a couple named Phil and Lola Jemson put on a good feed and clean bedding for the passengers at a reasonable price. Longarm took Trent outside, where they could talk privately, and then told him about the conversation that he'd had with Charley.

"Holy smoke!" Trent cried. "The editor in Durango never bothered to mention that the fella I was replacing had been gunned down!"

"Well, he was," Longarm said. "So be careful."

"You think that I ought to get a new pistol?"

"Yes. A cartridge revolver as well as a shotgun. Keep the shotgun in your room. It will give you and your pretty young wife some valuable peace of mind."

"Why a shotgun?"

"Because it's so much easier to hit what you aim for at close range."

Trent couldn't hide his nervousness. "Marshal, please don't mention this conversation to Esther. If she knew what we were talking about, she'd become hysterical."

"I understand."

"I'd appreciate it if you'd help me pick out a derringer and shotgun in Durango."

"There's a real fine gunsmith that I know there and

he'll give us a good deal. Don't worry," Longarm said, "I'm sure that you'll never have to defend yourself, but it's wise to be prepared for the worst."

"I'm starting to think that we should have stayed in Denver where it's more civilized," Trent fretted.

"Give it a chance," Longarm suggested. "If you are honest and not trying to print lies, I'm sure that you will do just fine."

"They never told me that this kind of thing happened when I was studying journalism."

"I'm sure that they didn't," Longarm said, "but it does happen in the Wild West."

Longarm offered Trent more instructions on how to handle a six-shooter. Actually, the kid was surprisingly good for someone who had never even fired a pistol. "If you practice you'll soon be better than most," Longarm told the young Easterner. "You've plenty of natural ability."

"Don't tell that to my wife," Trent replied. "I guarantee you that she will *not* be reassured."

"All right."

The closer they got to Durango, the more nervous everyone on the stage became. On their last stop, they stayed in a stone house that had been built by an early ranching family that had been massacred by the Ute Indians over twenty years before. The couple who were running the station were Mr. and Mrs. Bert and Adele Trabert, an elderly couple who were neither gracious nor friendly. They set a poor table, and Charley bawled them out for being stingy.

"You folks get paid every month by the stage company just to keep up a hospitable stage station! And here you are skimpin' on everything from the bread to the potatoes! We're hungry, dammit! Now, I want a *huge* breakfast waiting for us all at daybreak or there is going to be hell to pay!''

The next morning, they did have a good breakfast, but Charley was still irritated. ''You folks had damn sure better start changin' the sheets and airin' out them old mattresses. They're loaded with ticks and fleas!''

The couple nodded submissively, and although Longarm was scratching like a dog and bitten in a dozen places, he almost felt sorry for them.

''Charley, you were pretty hard on those old folks,'' he said before they rolled out of the station.

''Well, they were hard on us,'' Charley complained. ''And if I'm going to get killed today, I want it to happen on a full stomach. Is that so much to ask?''

''No,'' Longarm said, taking his rifle and climbing up beside the driver, ''I guess it isn't.''

''The thing of it is,'' Charley said, ''I ain't afraid of dying, but I'd rather be counted among the living.''

''I guess most everyone would agree on that.''

''I'm sixty-three years old,'' Charley confided in him, ''and I've had my share of troubles, but all in all, it's been a good and an interesting life. Why, I remember—''

The rifle shot exploded from the rocks about fifty yards off to their left, and Charley reached up and slapped his forehead as if he were swatting a mosquito. His eyes rolled up into his head and he pitched forward with blood pouring from the hole in his skull.

Longarm dove for the reins, but he was too late, and the excited team of horses began to run. Drawing his gun, he looked in vain for a target. He could hear Miranda, Trent, and Esther shouting down in the coach.

A volley of rifle shots sent Longarm ducking for cover as the stage accelerated down the mountain road. Longarm took a deep breath, then pushed the dead driver out of the way and made a grab for the lines, but they were far out of his reach. He glanced back and saw five horsemen appear from the rocks and take up chase.

"Miranda! Trent!" Longarm shouted. "They're coming after us, so get ready to shoot!"

Longarm looked up ahead, and saw that the road bent to the right and then disappeared down a mountainside. He couldn't see what lay ahead past that, but he didn't think it looked very good. Most likely, they were going to overturn.

He heard gunfire from the coach, and wished he could join them, but he had to get the lines dragging on the ground. Longarm jumped down on the tongue of the stage and held on for dear life. The road was rough, and every time he started to make a grab for the lines, he nearly fell, almost being run over by the coach.

Damn! What a mess!

Longarm knew that he wasn't going to be able to grab the lines, and he doubted that he could leap on the back of the nearest horse and try to pull it to a stop, but there didn't seem to be any choice but to try.

Here goes, he thought, jumping.

Somehow, he did land on the back of the wheel horse, and then he grabbed the lines and started wrenching on them. The stage began to slow, but not before they careened into that sharp right turn. Longarm decided that the coach was not going to make it. He could feel the coach lean precariously toward the steep drop-off into a canyon, and he bellowed, "It's going over! Jump!"

And then, because he was a firm believer in taking his own good advice, Longarm also jumped.

Chapter 6

Longarm didn't remember hitting the steep shale-covered mountainside. But he did recall being airborne, and then tumbling for what seemed like forever, until he smashed into a pine tree at the bottom of the gorge. He must have lost consciousness for several minutes, because he was awakened by Miranda's pleas.

"Custis! Wake up, Custis!"

He didn't want to wake up or even open his eyes. His entire body throbbed with pain. And yet Miranda's voice was so urgent, he had little choice but to open his eyes and try to gather his wits.

"Custis, Esther is unconscious! She might be dying!"

He roused himself a little. "What . . . what about her husband?"

"He was knocked out too, but seems to be coming around. The ambushers are searching for us! What are we going to do!"

"Help me up."

Miranda got her arm around his waist, and she managed to help get him to his feet, where Longarm swayed unsteadily, trying his best to focus. He was about to say something when a rifle bullet clipped a nearby rock and sent both him and Miranda spilling sideways into the deep stream that flowed along the bottom of this gorge.

"They're going to kill us!" Miranda cried as she and Longarm sought cover among the rocks.

The icy shock of the mountain water did a lot to clear Longarm's mind and focus his vision. He reached for his side arm, only to discover that it was missing, no doubt lost during his long tumble down the mountainside.

"Miranda, do you have a gun?"

"No, but I saw that old Navy Colt of Trent's lying on the rocks just up the slope."

Longarm peered out from behind the rocks. He was beginning to shiver, for the air was cold in the shadowy gorge and they were wet. It was then that he saw the wreckage of the stage about two hundred yards upriver. Two of the four horses were alive and thrashing in their traces. One, a sorrel, kept slamming its head down against the rocks as if trying to commit suicide.

"Are they going to come down and try to finish us off?" Miranda asked.

"I expect so," Longarm said. "They'll want to loot the stagecoach, and once they've come that far, I figure they'll decide to come down here and pick over our bodies."

"But they saw us and know we are alive!"

"They're going to guess that we're hurt and not much of a problem," Longarm said. "What I've got to do is to reach that Navy Colt and then see if I can hunt up anything else that will shoot."

"What about your pocket derringer?"

Longarm reached into his vest pocket. The crystal of

his Ingersoll watch was shattered, but there was nothing wrong with his deadly little two-shot derringer. "Yeah," he said, "this will help, but what I wouldn't give for a rifle!"

"What are we going to do?"

Longarm watched the outlaws start down the mountainside toward the overturned stagecoach. *They* sure had rifles, and there was probably one still in the overturned and smashed stagecoach, but that wasn't going to do him any good because the outlaws would reach it first.

"I'm going to get Trent's pistol and then hunt for my own," Longarm decided out loud.

"But they'll see you and start shooting again!"

"I know, but I *must* have something better than a derringer in my hand when they come to finish us off."

"What can I do?"

"Try to wake up Trent," Longarm told her. "We're going to need to move downstream and find a good hiding place. There's no way that we can defend ourselves here."

"All right. Be careful!"

"I'll do my level best," Longarm assured her as he began to creep up through the jumble of rocks toward where Miranda had seen Trent's Navy Colt.

More shots rang out, but Longarm kept ducking for cover and working his way up the slope. He finally had a little stroke of good luck when he located his own pistol as well as Trent's Navy Colt. The two were resting less than ten feet apart.

"All right," Longarm growled as he checked both weapons and determined that they were still functional. "Now we've got a fighting chance!"

He zigzagged his way back down the slope to Miranda, dodging bullets every step of the way. Trent was fully conscious but dazed, and he was cradling his young wife in his arms with tears streaming down his cheeks.

Longarm glanced at Miranda, who said with a sob in her voice, "Esther just died. I think she must have broken her neck in the fall."

Cold fury washed over Longarm. Esther had been a fine young lady who wouldn't have hurt anyone. She'd deserved a whole lot better than this tragic fate, and Longarm felt partially responsible. He should have advised the Roes not to journey to Durango just because he was on board the coach. Charley Blue was dead, and now this girl. That was enough, gawddamm it!

"We've got to move downstream and find a place to ambush this bunch," Longarm said.

Trent looked up at him, eyes brimming with tears. "I can't *leave* Esther!"

"You're going to have to," Longarm gently told the grieving young man.

"No!"

Longarm knelt beside Trent and placed his hand on the journalist's shoulder. "Look, I'm sorry about this, but getting yourself killed is not going to bring Esther back and it's not what she would want you to do."

"Custis is right," Miranda said. "She'd want you to try and survive this nightmare . . . just like you'd want her to survive if you'd been killed instead."

Trent choked deep in his throat. He looked up at Longarm, and then stared at the pistols he held in his hand. "You found my Navy Colt. Give it to me!"

Longarm stepped back, shaking his head. "No," he decided out loud. "I don't think that would be a good idea given your state of mind."

Trent lunged for his pistol, but Longarm was too quick for him. "You come with us downstream and when we find a good place to make our stand, then I'll give the pistol back.''

''It's mine and I'm going to kill them!'' Trent screamed, jumping for the gun.

Longarm had no choice but to pistol-whip him across the top of his head. Not real hard. Not nearly hard enough to knock him out cold, but hard enough to drop Trent and convince him to stop his foolishness.

A rifle bullet whistled by them, and it was uncomfortably close. ''Let's help him up, Miranda. We're running out of time!''

Longarm could see that the outlaws had already reached the overturned stagecoach. One of them must have been at least half human, because he dispatched the two injured and suffering animals with rifle bullets to their heads.

''Let's go!'' Longarm said, grabbing Trent and helping Miranda support him as they hurried along the stream bank.

It was tough going. The brush was thick and the rocks were slippery. They kept falling and struggling along, searching for someplace to hide, or at least a good defensive position.

''There!'' Longarm said, pointing to a massive boulder that was bigger than a cabin and that diverted the entire stream around its sides. ''If we can reach the top, there's no way that they can flank us and we'll have a big advantage.''

Miranda stared up at the immense boulder, which was at least twenty feet high. ''How in the world are we supposed to climb that given the bad shape we're in?''

A random bullet fired by the outlaws punctuated the urgency of their situation. Longarm knew full well that the gang would be coming, if they were not coming already.

"I dunno. Maybe we can't," Longarm replied as his eyes searched every inch of the giant boulder, seeking a crevice or some footholds that would allow them to scale the monolith, but finding nothing. "Let's wade into the stream and around the rock. Could be there's a way up on the downstream side."

The water channeled swiftly around the boulder. So swiftly that, when they tried to flank it, they were swept off their feet and spun around like leaves on a pond. Fortunately, they could all swim, and the current died as soon as it passed the giant rock. Longarm managed to keep his guns dry, especially the old Navy Colt, whose black powder would be useless had it been soaked.

"Look! We can climb up that fissure to the top."

"*You* can, but I can't and I'm sure that Trent can't either, thanks to that pistol you used on his head."

"He would have gotten himself killed," Longarm said, detecting accusation in Miranda's voice. "There was no other way to change his mind in a hurry."

"Oh?" Miranda didn't look convinced, but Longarm had neither the time nor the patience to argue the point.

"Are you sure that you can't make it to the top?" Longarm asked.

"Positive."

"All right, then. I'll go myself and try to take out as many as possible. You and Trent keep moving downstream just as fast as you can. If you see a good hiding place, try to reach it by first wading in the water to wash away your tracks."

"I thought you were—"

"There's five of them, Miranda. They've got rifles

and I've got just a pair of pistols. I might not be able to stop all of them. So go on!''

Miranda forgot about being angry at him for pistol-whipping Trent. She threw her arms around Longarm's neck and hugged him tightly. ''I don't want to leave you to face them alone.''

''It's best,'' he said. ''I'm the one that can put every bullet where I mean to, and we've none to waste. So go on before they show up.''

''I've got a derringer too,'' she said. ''When the shots were fired, I took it out of my purse and put it in my dress pocket. It's still there, and I won't hesitate to use it.''

''Let's just hope that you don't have to do that,'' Longarm replied, not wanting to even think about what this kind of men would do to a woman like Miranda if she fell into their clutches.

''I want to stay too,'' Trent said groggily.

''Get him out of here before I have to give him another hit across the head,'' Longarm warned.

Miranda dragged the still-dazed Trent after her. Longarm was afraid that the young man had suffered a serious head injury. Probably a concussion. He was in no shape to use a gun, and was likely seeing double.

When they were gone, Longarm holstered his own gun and wedged Trent's old percussion pistol under his belt, then began to climb up the fissure, knowing that it was absolutely imperative that he reach the top before the gang appeared. He was quite sure that he could kill at least two in the first volley, but after that, it was anyone's guess what would happen. At the very least, he could hold them off until after dark. Then he would climb down from this big rock and try to find Miranda and Trent and lead them far enough down canyon to safety.

That, at least, was his plan, but it wasn't one that gave him any great confidence. It was just the best that he could do under the circumstances.

Longarm had one hell of a bad time scaling the boulder. Miranda and Trent would never have made it. Most likely, they'd have fallen, because the rock was wet, slimy, and crumbly. It kept breaking away under Longarm's feet, sending showers of rock cascading into the stream below. Longarm didn't even want to think of descending the rock in the darkness. That would be almost impossible. What time was it? Mid-afternoon. Perhaps four o'clock. There would be another two or three hours of daylight at least.

Longarm crabbed his way across the crown of the boulder, staying low and moving as quickly as possible. It was capped with lichen and moss, and squishy to the touch. The entire gorge seemed to be shrouded in mist from this vantage point, and Longarm shivered in his wet clothing as the beginnings of a cool afternoon wind flowed down canyon.

The gang wouldn't be far behind. He hated to think of them with Esther's unprotected body. It seemed a sacrilege that they might even lay a hand on her while she lay there with a broken neck, pretty brown eyes staring up at eternity. Stop it, Longarm thought, there was no choice. We'd be dead by now if we'd stayed there to try to protect her body. What is important now is to protect the living. Especially Miranda. Dammit! I should never have let her talk me into allowing her to come!

Yet, even as Longarm argued with himself, he knew that he really hadn't had any choice. Miranda had insisted on coming and she had been right—it was a free country.

"Come on!" he said aloud, clenching his teeth to keep them from chattering. "Let's get this over with!"

Longarm inspected his guns once more. Especially the Navy Colt. He'd fired percussion pistols like this for years, but he wouldn't have imagined that his life would again depend on one. They were not very dependable in the rain or in this damned dampness. The Navy might shoot straight and fire correctly. Then again, it might not. Thank goodness he had found his own six-gun! Longarm had plenty of extra bullets in his cartridge belt, and he was very sure that he could hold off the outlaws until dark. Maybe, if he got very, very lucky, he could even kill or wound three of them. If he could do that, the other pair would surely call off the hunt and scurry out of this damned deep gorge before dark. Ambushers were, by the very nature of their act, a cowardly lot. They were men not given to bravery or risking their lives for anything but easy gain.

He had not waited more than a few minutes when he saw the leader cautiously emerge from behind a rock some thirty yards downstream. The man was big and made an inviting target. Longarm lay flat on the crown of his boulder and waited, wanting all of the gang members to be out in the open before he commenced to fire. He knew that he would only have a second or two to exploit his advantage of surprise, and he did not want to squander it on just one outlaw.

But the leader was smart. He saw the huge boulder, and must have realized it was an excellent ambush point. So he motioned his friends to stay behind cover. There was nothing that Longarm could do about that. He had no choice but to let the leader pass out of sight behind the safety of rocks very near his own boulder. But damned if he would allow any more of them to have the same safe passage.

The leader must have given his men a signal that they should come ahead because, suddenly, all four came into view. They were not cautious. They didn't glance up at the boulder where Longarm waited, nor did they seem to be in any hurry, which was easy enough to understand. After all, how much of a threat could their quarry be after being trapped in a stagecoach that had rolled down a mountainside? The outlaws probably figured that the survivors were badly injured and scared out of their wits.

Longarm had already decided to use his own pistol first because that was the one that he trusted. He took aim on the first outlaw and fired, nailing him squarely in the chest. In less than a second, Longarm shot a second outlaw, his slug knocking the man over backward into the stream. The third and fourth outlaws wheeled and ran for their lives but Longarm was able to get off one last shot. His slug struck one of them in the hip and spun him around. Longarm would have finished him off, but the wounded outlaw had the good fortune of falling between some rocks, howling like a dying dog.

Longarm grinned with satisfaction. "Three down and just two to go!"

Longarm waited. The wounded man kept screaming, his cries echoing up and down the deep, misty gorge. Longarm reloaded his own gun and stayed right where he was. If the leader was attempting to climb this rock, then he was a dead man, because he couldn't do it without dislodging pebbles and rocks and making one hell of a racket.

"Come on," Longarm whispered, staring at the place

where the fifth man had taken cover. "Your friend is screaming his head off and probably bleeding to death! Don't just sit there listening."

As if his words were heard, the last outlaw poked his head up and then, very slowly, emerged. The man was a fool. He unleashed three blind shots up toward where Longarm lay in wait, then sprinted over to his wounded friend, grabbed him under the arms, and tried to haul him to safer cover. Longarm shot the fool in the head, and he fell twitching on the wet sand while his wounded friend lay screaming.

"Four down and one to go," Longarm whispered to himself as he eased backward, then turned and crawled across the crown of the boulder to the deep fissure that he had used to gain this vantage point.

He peered downward and saw nothing at first. No movement. Nothing. So he gave the outlaw leader a few minutes more. Patience, Longarm had discovered, was about the most difficult but most important thing for either a hunter or someone hunted to learn. Animals understood patience. Indians did too. But a white man . . . well, very few other than the old mountain men possessed any patience. Longarm liked to think of himself as one of the few notable exceptions.

"Come on," Longarm urged the leader, who was still hiding somewhere below.

The leader was not only cautious, he was uncommonly patient. Had Longarm not been able to have a clear view upstream and know that the man was not going after Miranda and Trent, he would have felt compelled to climb down from the rock. But he *did* have a clear view, and so he sat still and waited.

Finally, he heard the sound of pebbles and loose rocks being dislodged, and knew that the leader was coming up to get him. Longarm smiled coldly. His teeth were chattering again. He wished for a smoke and a warming fire. But he would have neither until this business was completed.

Now he could hear the grunts and gasping of the climber, punctuated by stretches of silence as the man waited and listened for danger.

Come on, just a little farther.

The leader finally appeared. He had been forced to holster his gun because he needed both hands to climb. Longarm inched up to the edge of the rock, pointed his gun directly down into the leader's face, and said, "Surprise!"

The leader started to reach for his gun, and Longarm shot him in the hand. The man screamed as blood pumped from the wound. Then he cried, "Don't kill me!"

"Then unholster your gun by reaching for it with your left hand."

"If I do, I'll fall!"

"If you don't, I'll shoot."

The outlaw wedged himself into the fissure as tight as a possible, then removed and dropped his gun.

"All right," Longarm said, "you can start down slowly just the same way you came up."

"I don't think I can make it. Not with one hand out of commission."

"Give it your best effort," Longarm said without a trace of sympathy. "Either way, it makes no difference to me."

The leader started backing down, and Longarm noted that, bullet-riddled hand or not, the man was going to do everything in his power to safely reach the streambed below. Longarm figured he'd probably make it, and then when he did, he'd make a grab for his fallen pistol and try to shoot Longarm.

It made a lot of sense. Longarm would then be the one at a big disadvantage. *I ought to just shoot him and be done with it. After all, he gave Charley no warning. He and his outlaw friends shot Charley from ambush knowing that the coach would go over the side of the mountain and probably kill everyone inside. Go ahead and kill him, Custis!*

But Longarm couldn't. He'd never executed anyone. He'd taken an oath to uphold the law, not live by his own law. So he stopped his own descent and slowly turned with his gun pointed down at the leader. And sure enough, when the man jumped to the streambed below, the very first thing he did was grab his fallen pistol, roll over onto his back, and look up with every intent to blow Longarm off the rock.

Longarm drilled the man twice. Then, holstering his own gun, he very carefully descended the slippery fissure until his feet were again on solid ground.

All the outlaws were dead except for the one with a bullet in his hip, and he was dying from internal bleeding.

To hell with him, Longarm thought, remembering Esther's dead, staring eyes as he hurried upstream. To hell with them all.

Chapter 7

Longarm found Miranda and Trent holed up under some boulders less than a quarter of a mile downstream. Like himself, they were shaking from the cold.

"What happened?" Miranda asked.

"They won't be bothering us anymore," Longarm answered, not wanting to elaborate.

"You killed *all* of them?" Trent asked with an expression of disbelief written on his pale, bruised face.

"I had the advantage of surprise and luck was with me," Longarm explained. "But our troubles are far from over. We've got to figure out our next move. We need food as well as warm, dry clothes."

"It seems obvious to me that we have to go back to the stagecoach," Miranda said. "We need to get our bags and extra dry clothes. There's also some food, if it wasn't thrown out on the way down the mountainside."

"I agree." Longarm looked up at the sky. "It will be dark soon. We can camp beside the stage and build a roaring good fire. Maybe someone traveling the road above will see our fire or smell the smoke and look over the side. We definitely need help.''

"I won't leave Esther alone again,'' Trent vowed, his voice as dead as his wife. ''I won't do it.''

"Of course not,'' Longarm replied, worried about the man's mental state. ''We'll carry her body out and see that she gets a proper burial in Durango.''

"Maybe she'd want to be sent back to her hometown,'' Trent protested.

"No,'' Longarm told the grieving man, ''she'd rather be buried in Colorado near where you are staying.''

Trent didn't agree, but he didn't disagree either. Longarm helped them both out of their hiding place, and they walked back upstream, skirting the giant boulder and seeing the dead outlaw leader lying on his back with two crimson stains on his shirtfront.

"Are we just going to leave him like this?'' Trent asked.

"What else can we do?'' Miranda responded. ''You weren't thinking of burying the man, were you?''

"But there are wild animals around and it is possible that they could—''

"Look,'' Longarm said, ''our first obligation is survival. Later, I can send a party down here to recover the bodies and see that they are properly buried. But for now, let's just push on back to the coach and make ourselves as warm and comfortable as possible.''

Longarm led the way back upstream, and when he came to the dying man he'd shot in the hip, Trent again objected, saying, ''We can't just leave this man here alone.''

"Then *you* carry him all the way back up to the coach,'' Longarm snapped. ''Because I don't have the time or the inclination to do it myself.''

"I'll stay with him," Miranda offered. "A man shouldn't have to die alone."

"Suit yourself," Longarm replied. "I'll go up and see what I can find in the stage that will help us get through the night. I'll build a fire and then come back down for you when I've done as much as I can."

"I'll go with you," Trent said. "My first obligation is to my wife."

"No," Longarm corrected, "your first obligation is to take care of yourself and try to be useful. That's what your wife would say."

"You are right," Trent agreed, "it is. And I suppose that it will get pretty cold down in this canyon tonight."

"It will freeze. Trent, we're going to need to collect a lot of firewood in order to keep dry and warm."

Trent nodded with understanding, and Longarm was grateful. He had seen a lot of people who had lost someone they loved deeply, and knew that the best medicine was to keep them busy. Longarm would see that Trent was the wood collector and that he also was responsible for feeding tonight's fire.

"Be back in about an hour!" Longarm called to Miranda, who had sat down beside the dying outlaw. "You stay back from that snake or he's likely to try and kill you."

"I will," Miranda promised as she moved back even further out of the dying man's reach.

Longarm hurried up to the coach, and then he quickly emptied it of everything useful including its curtains and cushions. There were no blankets, but at least they could wear all of their extra clothes. Besides, a fire would make all the difference in the world.

Trent spent some time beside the body of his young wife, and Longarm had to chide him into action. Finally,

75

the kid began to gather armfuls of the readily available driftwood and stack it on a sandy beach. Longarm, meanwhile, took all the baggage out of the overturned coach and piled it neatly aside. His own bags had been rifled by the outlaws, but there didn't appear to be much of anything missing. He changed out of his wet clothes into dry ones, and immediately felt better. He was glad that his things had not been sacked. No doubt the outlaws had been looking for valuables, and would have conducted a more thorough and extensive looting after they had disposed of the passengers.

"Trent?"

"Yes?"

"I want you to change into some dry clothes. You won't be any good to anyone if you catch pneumonia."

"Now?"

"That's right. Change right now."

"All right."

Longarm searched the area, and even climbed a little ways up the mountainside, searching to see if anything else could be found that might be of use. But he found nothing. He would remove the weapons and any valuables from the dead outlaws, and the money they had could be spent on helping Trent give his wife a handsome funeral.

The canyon shadows had begun to deepen when Longarm decided that it was time to go retrieve Miranda. The last thing he wanted was to be caught fumbling around in darkness after the sun went down. But there would be almost a full moon out tonight, and that would be some help.

"Trent, I'll start a fire now. You stay close and make sure that it doesn't get out of control."

"Sure. But first, let me go get Esther's body and bring

her over here. I want her resting in the firelight, not lying out there in the dark, cold and alone. You can understand that, can't you, Marshal?''

"Of course I can. I'll help you.''

"No,'' Trent said in a way that left no room for argument, "I'd rather do it myself.''

"All right. I'm going back for Miranda now.''

"What if that outlaw you shot in the hip is still alive? You can't just leave him to die!''

Longarm started to remind the young Easterner that it was entirely possible that the wounded man had shot Charley in the head without even giving him fair warning or a chance to surrender. But then Longarm decided to just keep his grim words to himself.

"I'll handle it,'' Longarm said, starting to leave.

"You can't just *shoot* him!''

"No,'' Longarm said, "I can't. But it's my business, not yours, so get your wife's body over by the fire and sit tight. I won't be gone long.''

"All right,'' Trent replied.

Longarm hurried back downstream. He found Miranda just where he had left her, and sat down on the same rotting log. "How is he?''

"He's almost dead,'' Miranda replied. "He told me that his name was George Goddard, and he said that the one that tried to save him was his older brother Jeff. He said he was sorry for all the bad things they'd done, and asked me to pray for him and his poor brother.''

"Well,'' Longarm said, going over to touch the man's wrist and see if there was still a pulse, "I'm glad he asked *you*, because I'd have told him that he could go straight to Hell without the comfort of my prayers.''

"You're not a very forgiving man, are you.''

"Not when it comes to murderers, thieves, and ambushers," Longarm answered, discovering that George's heart had stopped beating. "Miranda, he's gone."

"Are you sure?"

"Yes. I am."

She came over and checked George's pulse for herself. He saw that her teeth were chattering from the cold, and he knew that she was going to become ill if she didn't get into dry clothes and get warm beside their fire. "All right, I guess we can go back to the stagecoach now," he said. "You need to get warm and dry."

"How is Trent doing?"

"Not well."

"He really loved Esther."

"I know. She was a fine girl."

"Custis, she told me that she was only twenty years old. That's so very young to die." A sob escaped Miranda's lips, and she began to cry.

"Come on," he said gently as he led her back upstream.

It was nearly dark by the time they arrived at their survival campsite. Trent was seated cross-legged beside his wife's body, his hand resting on her shoulder. He was staring into the flames with an expression of such profound sadness that Longarm hated to look at the man.

"Miranda," Longarm said, "I've got your bags laid out over here. I want you to change into some dry clothes and then come and sit close to the fire."

"Did you find that basket of food that we were nibbling on yesterday?"

"No," Longarm said. "I guess that it must have fallen out up near the top of mountainside. I'm going up now, though."

Miranda and Trent both seemed to snap out of a daze,

and it was Trent who said, "You can't go now. It's dark and you could—"

"I need to catch up with the outlaws' horses, if that is still possible," Longarm explained. "I'll tether them up so they will be waiting for us in the morning when we climb out together. We'll need horses in order to reach Durango and help."

"I'll come with you," Miranda offered.

"No," Longarm replied, going to the stream and drinking his fill of the icy mountain water. "Miranda, you really need to stay here and conserve your energy for what will be a difficult climb out tomorrow morning."

Miranda was distraught, but she was still reasonable. "Yes, I suppose that I do."

It took Longarm nearly an hour to scale the steep mountainside and reach the road high above. It had been a tough climb mainly because the footing was so loose with shale. It seemed as if, for every yard he climbed, he would slide back a foot or two. By the time Longarm got to the road, he was trembling with fatigue. The sun had gone down, and it was completely dark except for moon and starlight.

At first his heart sank, for he could see no sign of the outlaws' horses. But after walking up and down the road for a short distance, he heard one of them nicker somewhere off in the brush, and then he quickly found the animals. All five horses were securely tied where they could not have been seen by anyone just passing down the road.

"Easy, easy," Longarm said as one of the horses snorted and began to pull back on its tie rope. "I'm not here to hurt you, so just take it easy."

The animals were calmed by his gentleness. Longarm

untied all of the saddlebags and searched them, finding plenty of jerked beef, bread, corn, and even some cheap whiskey. He stuffed the food into one of the saddlebags until it bulged, and then he slung it all over his shoulder.

"I'm sorry that I can't water you horses tonight," he said, knowing that the animals would be both hungry and thirsty. "But we'll be up at first light and then we'll see that you get water."

Longarm hurried back into the gorge with his bounty. He slipped so often that he finally just sat down and sledded on the shifting shale until he reached the bottom, then hurried over to his friends.

"We're in luck," he said, emptying the saddlebags and handing food to Miranda and Trent. "We'll not go hungry, that's for sure."

"How are the horses?" Miranda asked.

"They'll be waiting when we climb out tomorrow."

"I won't leave Esther," Trent said again.

"We'll carry her out some way," Longarm assured the man. "Don't worry about that."

"Okay."

They all felt much better after they had eaten. Miranda huddled up close by Longarm, and they fell asleep by their bonfire. Trent didn't sleep, though. At least not much because, each time Longarm roused in the night, he glanced over and saw the young man staring into the fire.

Longarm wished that he could give the man some comfort, but he knew that his words would have no impact whatsoever. Trent was probably blaming himself for allowing them both to come to the West, and especially to risk taking the stagecoach to Durango in the face of almost certain danger. Longarm knew that guilt could be a terrible cross to bear. Maybe there would be a preacher in Durango who could offer Trent some comfort after they arrived.

In the morning, they ate quickly, and then Longarm spent a quarter of an hour making a litter out of the stagecoach's leather curtains and the leather reins that he cut from the dead horses.

"It's going to be rough," he told Trent. "But we'll just take our time and we'll make it. Lead off, Miranda, and we'll follow."

Trying to haul the litter with Esther's body strapped to it up the steep and difficult mountainside was a job that Longarm hoped never to repeat. It took them nearly all morning, and they were exhausted by the time they finally made it to the wagon road high above.

Afterward, Longarm tightened saddle cinches. They tied Esther across the back of one saddle, and Charley Blue's body across another, before they continued on toward Durango. They were all filthy and bedraggled. Longarm was worried about Trent doing something crazy, for the young Easterner did not say even one word and seemed nearly comatose with grief.

"We'll be in Durango before nightfall," Longarm said, hoping that that bit of news would cheer them up a little.

It didn't, and so they rode on until they found a stream where the thirsty horses could drink their fill. There was grass there too, and Longarm tied ropes to the animals and allowed them to graze for an hour before they pushed on.

Late that afternoon, they met a wagon heading for Pueblo. When the driver saw them, he quickly realized that something was terribly wrong.

"We were attacked by the outlaw gang that has been

preying on the stagecoaches,'' Longarm said.

"And you survived!"

"That's right."

"You people look like you've been through Hell. Whose bodies are those tied—"

Trent exploded, "Why don't you just button your gawdamm flapping lip, mister!"

The stranger looked at Trent's tear-streaked face and said, "Yeah, I'm sorry. I'll tell 'em what happened to the stage when I reach Pueblo."

"Thanks," Longarm said. "Tell them that there were five outlaws and their bodies are still down in the canyon."

"I'll do that. Durango ain't but a couple of hours farther on," the driver said as he slapped the lines on the rumps of his horses and drove away.

Longarm studied young Roe. "Are you all right?"

"No," Trent said, "but I'm not going to go crazy, if that's what you are worried about."

"It isn't," Longarm lied.

"At least," Miranda said, "that gang won't be looting or murdering anyone else."

"That's right," Longarm said, appreciating how Miranda was trying to see the one bright side of this tragic situation.

Chapter 8

When Longarm, Miranda, and Trent Roe rode up the streets of Durango, people came out of the saloons and other shops to stare at them. It was not surprising really, considering their appearance and the fact that they had two bodies tied across saddles.

"The marshal's office is just up the street," Longarm said, reining in at the town's only undertaker. "After we make the arrangements for Charley and Esther, I'll go pay him a visit and explain what happened to the stage."

But Longarm had hardly dismounted when the marshal arrived and introduced himself as Seth Palladin, saying, "We expected that your stagecoach ran into trouble when it didn't arrive on schedule."

Palladin was a heavyset man in his early thirties with a long flowing mustache, an orange silk tie, starched white shirt, embroidered vest, and fancy boots. He wore an ivory-handled Colt, and appeared far more prosperous than most frontier marshals. Longarm figured that the man had probably come from a prominent local family, or else had married into one.

"Then I'm surprised that you didn't send out a posse to investigate," Longarm said, for he had expected them to be met long before they reached Durango.

Palladin didn't like that remark, and his mustache actually bristled. "Well," he huffed, "we'd have come on out, but I've got this here town to protect. These people are the ones that pay my salary, not the stage line."

"All the same," Longarm said, "there might have been some of your voters aboard that stage and you are the authority in this area, aren't you?"

Palladin's jaw muscles corded. It seemed to Longarm that the man was acutely aware of the gathering crowd that was watching how he handled this trouble.

"Mister," Palladin said, "I don't know who in the hell you think you are to be talking to me that way, but we need to step into my office and have a *private* conversation. There are some things that you have a crying need to be educated about."

"That suits me just fine," Longarm replied. He turned to Miranda. "My dear, why don't you help Trent out and I'll be back before long."

"Are you sure?" Miranda had not missed the anger in Palladin's voice and looked concerned. "Maybe I should—"

"Ma'am," the marshal said, "who are you?"

"She's my wife," Longarm said in a flat, hard voice. "And I'll speak for her. This whole business has been very upsetting. I'm sure you understand."

"Follow me," Palladin commanded, tipping his hat to Miranda and then wheeling around to head for his office.

"I already dislike that man," Miranda whispered to Longarm before he left. "Haven't we had enough trouble without having to deal with someone who thinks all this might have happened just so that you can show him up?''

"I've dealt with his kind plenty often," Longarm answered, "and I know how to handle him. Just stay with Trent, and I'll get Marshal Palladin set straight."

Longarm had to really stretch his legs in order to catch up with the marshal. The man was angry and moving fast.

"Close the door behind you," Palladin ordered after they had entered his office, "and then have a seat across from my desk. I want to know *every* damned detail from start to finish, and don't leave anything out because it may be important to my investigation."

"Have you got an election coming up soon?" Longarm asked, easing into a rickety chair of his own choosing.

"Dammit!" Palladin shouted. "You're starting to get under my skin."

"Look," Longarm said, curbing his own temper, "why don't we just start over and let me explain that I'm—"

"I'll ask the damned questions! You answer the questions! Is that plain enough?"

Longarm had heard enough. He reached into his pocket and drew out his United States deputy marshal's badge, then tossed it on the lawman's desk.

"Is that plain enough for *you*, Marshal Palladin?" he demanded in a hard voice.

The transformation in Palladin was immediate and remarkable. "Well, why the hell didn't you say right off that you were a federal officer instead of letting me think that you were just someone passing through who had the bad luck to get on the wrong stagecoach?"

"You didn't give me a chance to explain, and I didn't

85

want to tell the whole damn town. I'm here incognito," Longarm said. "I've been sent on official business and I would prefer that my real identity be kept a secret."

Palladin snorted with derision. "Well, that's going to be a hell of a neat trick, considering that you announced yourself with two dead bodies."

"Look," Longarm said, fighting to preserve his composure. "We were attacked about twenty miles east of town yesterday afternoon. There were five in the gang and they ambushed and killed our driver, Charley Blue."

"I never liked Charley."

Longarm ignored the remark and kept on talking. "Our runaway coach went over the side of a mountain, and it was a miracle that we were not all crushed. As it was, a very fine woman, Esther Roe, died from her injuries. That young man you saw with us is her husband Trent. He has been hired by your local newspaper."

Palladin made a face. "Hell, he don't look old enough to be taking on a job like that! I don't suppose that anyone bothered to tell him what happened to our last reporter, who was just about as wet behind the ears."

"Trent knows that story," Longarm said, "and it would be nice if you'd try to put yourself in his position. He's just lost his wife and he's pretty much in shock. But I think if people will give him a little time, he'll snap out of it and make a fine reporter. I can vouch for the fact that young Trent Roe has character."

"To be real honest," Palladin said, waving his big hand, "I don't care one damned way or the other what happens to him. But I *do* care about getting to the bottom of this ambush and stage holdup."

"Good! I'm delighted to hear that, because the stage and all five of the outlaws who waylaid it are still resting at the bottom of the gorge where we landed. I suggest you form a posse that will double as a burial party and go see what happened for yourself."

Palladin didn't seem very keen on that idea. He frowned, then rolled a cigarette. After making a show of lighting it and blowing a big smoke ring overhead, he kicked his feet up on his desk and said, "I'll send out a couple of boys to bury them outlaws where they lay and check out your story."

Longarm ignored the insult. "Two of the outlaws were brothers. One was named George Goddard and his brother was named Jeff. Do you know them?"

"Sure! Their old man, Luke Goddard, owns a little spread up in Six Mile Canyon just about twelve miles southwest of here. He's a small-time cattle rustler and a wild bastard when he gets drunk and decides to raise hell. The whole family is a tough bunch, and I've been at odds with them ever since I took office. Clyde, one of the clan, actually campaigned against me trying to get my job, if you can believe that."

"It would not have been the first time that an outlaw family tried to buy into legitimacy by winning an electoral office. I think that you and I ought to ride out there and have a talk with the Goddard family. Better that they hear the news of it from us than from someone else."

"Luke will go crazy when we tell him you shot two of his favorite sons. If I were you, Marshal, I'd grab that Eastern kid and make fast tracks out of Durango before the Goddard clan hears the news and comes looking for you."

"I don't run," Longarm said. "I never run."

"Then you are likely to get shot."

Longarm's eyebrows lifted in question. "Am I to understand that you'd just step aside and allow that to happen?"

Palladin threw up his hands in a gesture of hopelessness. "What other choice would I have?"

"You'd have plenty of choice," Longarm snapped. "You took an oath to serve and protect."

"Serve and protect my *townsfolk,* not some quick-on-the-trigger federal officer who arrives in Durango bearing me a piss pot full of grief."

Longarm had heard more than enough, and came to his feet. "I think this conversation is over."

"What is your business in this town?"

"That is none of your business, Palladin. And besides, we'll be leaving for Cortez just as soon as I can make the arrangements."

"I like the sound of that. And like I said, I ain't anxious to get crossways of Luke Goddard. To prevent that, I'll even help you hire a buggy or some saddle horses so that you and your friends leave within the hour."

Longarm didn't like the way this conversation was going. Didn't like it at all. Time permitting, he would have stayed in Durango and straightened Palladin out. Furthermore, he would have bet money that Old Man Goddard was involved with his sons holding up stage coaches and that he could find evidence to support this theory out at their ranch.

Maybe, after Billy Vail's assignment was finished, he would return to Durango and pay the Goddards a visit when they least expected it.

"I can make my own travel arrangements," Longarm told Palladin when he stopped beside his door. "But I'll tell you this. If word gets out that I'm really a federal marshal, then I'll know who to blame."

"Now wait just a damned minute!"

"No," Longarm said, "*you* wait. It's clear that we aren't going to be friends and I can accept that. But what

I won't accept is you interfering with my job by flapping your mouth and telling people who I really am."

Palladin was almost livid with anger. "Are you threatening me, Marshal?"

"Yeah," Longarm answered, "I guess that I am."

"I could make a lot of trouble for you. You've got no friends here. You don't understand. . . ."

Longarm had been heading out the door, but now he turned and marched back to Palladin, reached over his desk, and yanked the man to his feet. "Don't *ever* threaten me with trouble! You do that and I'll arrest you for obstructing a federal officer, and then I'll have you behind bars in Denver faster than you can say 'dammit.' Is that understood?"

Palladin didn't understand anything. He was almost as tall as Longarm, and outweighed him by at least fifteen pounds. Furthermore, he was a man accustomed to bullying and intimidating other men.

Longarm gazed into Palladin's eyes for an instant, and he saw fight rather than fear. Palladin reared back, tearing free of Longarm's grasp, and then he came charging around his desk, murder written all over his square face.

Palladin threw a straight right at Longarm's jaw, but missed. Longarm stepped inside and drove a punishing uppercut to the heavier man's gut. Palladin's mouth flew open like a fish out of water. Longarm filled that gaping mouth with his knuckles, and Palladin crashed over backward, striking the floor so hard that it shook.

"Get up," Longarm ordered.

Palladin wiped his bloody mouth and shook his head. "Another time," he wheezed. "This ain't settled yet."

"You're right about that. When I'm through with the business that I came out here to settle, I'll be passing back through Durango, and you can bet that I'll be pay-ing you a visit that you're not going to enjoy.''

Palladin climbed unsteadily to his feet, holding his gut. He was ashen-faced, and Longarm knew that he was in pain.

"Come back through *my* town," Palladin swore, "and you are writing your own death warrant.''

Longarm took a menacing step forward. "Are you saying you'll *kill* me?''

"No," Palladin said, spitting blood on the floor. "But then I'm a man with a lot of friends and favors owed.''

Longarm took a short step forward and dropped the local marshal with a straight right cross to his jaw.

"I'll be back," he vowed. "And if you know what is good for you, you'll be long gone.''

When he rejoined Miranda outside the undertaker's office, she immediately noticed that his knuckles were bleeding. "What happened!''

"Marshal Palladin and I had a little dispute over a matter of authority," Longarm told her. "How is Trent holding up?''

"Not well. He's inside with the undertaker, a man named Otis Palmer. I think Trent could use some help.''

"I'll see what I can do," Longarm said, going inside.

Otis Palmer was small, nervous, and wore a dirty black suit that had seen far better days. In his fifties, he had a twitch under his right eye and the most delicate hands that Longarm had ever seen on a man.

"Mr. Roe," the undertaker was saying, "I simply can't give your wife the kind of funeral you want for eighteen dollars. Now, there is nothing wrong with a pine casket, and we can—''

"You have a problem here?'' Longarm asked.

Trent looked to be in a daze, and Longarm could see at once that the young man was near the breaking point.

He took Trent's arm and led him outside, saying, "Stay here with Miranda and I'll take care of the arrangements."

"He wants more money than I have left," Trent said quietly.

"I'll take care of it," Longarm repeated. "Miranda?"

Miranda took the young man aside, and Longarm went back into the funeral parlor to see the undertaker. He was in no mood to haggle, and came right to the point. "What's the problem?"

"The young man wants to buy a first-class funeral on a pauper's purse," Palmer answered. "I can't even buy the kind of casket he wants for eighteen dollars!"

"How much then?"

"For what?"

"For everything it takes to give that girl a first-class funeral?"

"Thirty-five dollars to me, but then the flowers will cost extra and . . ."

"Here," Longarm said, reaching into his pocket and dragging out some bills. "Fifty dollars. Do it up right. The best of everything."

"Yes, sir!" Palmer replied, brightening up considerably. "And I must tell you that it will be a pleasure. She was a lovely girl and died much too . . ."

But Longarm wasn't listening. Instead, he was heading outside to rejoin Trent and Miranda. In a very few words, he told them about his trouble with Palladin, and ended by saying, "Trent, why don't you go get a hotel room. You need some rest."

"What about you and Miranda?"

"We're leaving for Cortez."

"Can't you even stay for the funeral?"

"I'm afraid that won't be possible," Longarm said.

"I wish I could, but I just cannot. Orders are orders."

"Sure," Trent said. "Did you make Mr. Palmer understand what I want for Esther?"

"Yes. Don't worry about it. All the arrangements are taken care of and she'll have a fine funeral."

"Thank you," Trent said. "And good-bye."

"Good-bye," Longarm replied. "And good luck with your new job. If you have any trouble, you can reach me in Cortez."

"I'll be fine. It will just take time to heal. A lot of time."

"That's the spirit," Miranda said, her eyes damp with tears. "And we'll be sure and stop by to visit you when we come back through town."

"Thanks."

Longarm hated to leave the young man, but he was anxious to be on their way to Cortez. The sooner he got there and completed his assignment, the sooner he could return and look in to make sure that Trent was adjusting to his new life.

"I wish we could at least stay over long enough to attend Esther's funeral," Miranda said as he led her toward the livery, where he intended to rent them horses or a buggy.

"Can you ride a horse?"

"Sure. I'm an excellent rider."

"Than let's rent horses instead of a buggy," Longarm decided out loud.

"But I'll need a riding skirt."

"Go buy one and meet me back here in an hour," Longarm told her. "The sooner we get out of Durango, the better."

Miranda gave him a funny look, but Longarm had neither the will nor the inclination to go into a lengthy explanation. So she went off to buy a riding skirt, and he went into the livery to rent them a couple of decent horses.

"Howdy," the liveryman called in greeting. "What can I do for you today?"

"I need to rent a couple of good saddle horses."

"Why, then, you came to the right place! How long do you need them for?"

"Hard to say," Longarm answered. "My wife and I want to see the old cliff dwellings at Mesa Verde and then just ride around and enjoy ourselves for a while."

"Then I'll give you my *weekly* rate," the liveryman said, rubbing his hands together. "Be a dollar per animal per day. And that includes saddles, bridles, blankets, and even a halter and lead rope for each animal."

"Fair enough," Longarm said. "As long as they are quality horses. We don't want something that could go lame on us out on the trail."

"Oh, don't worry about that! I have a couple of good rental horses and both have recently been shod."

"Let's have a look," Longarm told the man.

They were bay geldings, and Longarm examined them closely. They were smooth-mouthed, so they weren't young, but then Longarm preferred mature animals because they were less spooky and more sensible. For a few extra dollars, the liveryman threw in tarps and some clean blankets.

"I'm afraid that I don't have any cooking utensils to rent," he told Longarm. "But I do have a pack burro that you might want to rent."

"No, thanks." Longarm paid the man for one week in advance, and then he helped saddle the animals.

"I'll take the shorter one," Miranda said when she arrived, already wearing her riding habit. Just then, a small Mexican burro came trotting out of the barn, braying piteously.

"Oh, how cute!" Miranda cried, hurrying over to throw her arms around the burro's neck.

"He's going to be mighty heartbroken when you take his *best* friends away," the liveryman lamented, appearing just as upset as the noisy burro. "I told your husband that I'd rent him to you for nearly nothing, but he said he didn't think that you'd need him."

"Why, sure we do!" Miranda cried, scratching the burro's long ears so that it stopped braying and sighed with contentment. "How are we supposed to get all our baggage down to Cortez without a cute little pack animal?"

"Maybe I should have rented a buckboard," Longarm growled.

"Naw," the liveryman said. "I'll let you have this little fella *and* a packsaddle, lead rope, and halter for only another fifty cents a day! Now, you won't get that kind of a price in Cortez. No, sir, those guides and such that take you up to the cliff dwellings and other ruins will gouge your eyes out for an extra nickel."

"We'll take him," Longarm said.

"That will be another three dollars and fifty cents for a week in advance," the man told him with a triumphant grin.

Longarm paid the fellow thinking that if he didn't stop spending cash, he would have to wire Billy for more right away. But that was all right too. This Anasazi problem had a very high priority in Denver, and Longarm figured that he could have all the time and expense money that he needed to get it solved.

Besides, the burro was sort of cute, and it was clearly attached to the two bay geldings he'd just rented. No sense in causing any more grief in this world than was necessary.

"How far is Cortez exactly?" Longarm asked the man.

"Just a little over thirty miles. You're not getting a very early start, and so I expect that you'll want to lay over tonight at the little town of Mancos. It's about halfway. Got a nice hotel and cafe there. Good people that will treat you right. Just tell them that Jason McFarland sent you along."

"I'll do that," Longarm said.

Fifteen minutes and a lightly loaded burro later, they rode out of town headed for Mancos. It was a fine day, and Longarm was glad to be back on the road, although he was a little worried about Trent Roe. As ornery as Marshal Palladin was, it crossed Longarm's mind that he might even decide to take out his anger on Trent for no better reason than he was Longarm's friend. *I should have warned him about not doing that,* Longarm thought as he led the way west.

Chapter 9

The little ranching and mining town of Mancos proved itself hospitable enough, and they got an early start for Cortez the next day. The southern Colorado mountain country was quite beautiful, and when they rode down into the high desert country that surrounded Cortez, Longarm was surprised to see how much it had grown since he'd passed through a few years earlier.

"This is mostly a ranching town, although there is some mining activity," Longarm explained. "And you can see that there are several outfits that take tour groups up to the cliff dwellings."

"I can hardly wait to see them," Miranda said. "Why don't we talk to a few of these tour groups after we board the horses and get a hotel room."

"I'll probably be needing a day or two before we leave to investigate," Longarm told her. "After all, I really don't expect to catch the Anasazi grave robbers in the act."

"Custis, you might get lucky and do exactly that."

But Longarm didn't think so. If the gang had any

common sense at all, they would be excavating during the off-season when there was very little likelihood of discovery. This country could get very cold in the winter, and deep snows were not uncommon. Longarm was quite sure that if you were caught up on Mesa Verde unprepared, you could freeze to death.

"Let's take care of these horses and just see how it goes," Longarm said. "That livery over there looks good to me."

The OK Livery was just about what you would expect in a town as small as Cortez. It had one large and drafty barn with private stalls inside and a tack room as well as a loft crammed with fresh summer hay. Outside were two or three corrals and several dozen wagons in various states of decay and disrepair. There was also a blacksmith's forge and anvil, which told Longarm that the liveryman was also a farrier.

"Howdy," a short and powerful man about Longarm's age called as he came to greet them. He was wearing a red flannel shirt and smoking a corncob pipe. "You be needing to put your horses and that ugly little burro up for a while?"

"He's *not* ugly," Miranda argued.

"Sorry, ma'am! Didn't mean for you to take it personal. Why, you're right! He is an uncommonly handsome little critter, given the state of his race."

Longarm quickly came to terms about the price of boarding. After helping to unsaddle and then unload their supplies and belongings, he said, "What hotel would you recommend for me and my wife?"

"There ain't but two, and one of them isn't fit for a lady," the liveryman said. "So that just leaves you with the Concord Hotel. It ain't nothin' to brag about, but it serves all the tourists and the food is pretty good. It's run by a spunky old widow woman named Mrs. Mc-Allister. Yes, sir! Jenny McAllister is a real corker!''

"What does that mean?" Longarm asked.

"It means that if she likes you, you couldn't ask for a better friend. But if she takes a dislike to you, then you'd be safer sleeping in a den full of rattlesnakes. The woman has quite a colorful past, which, I might add, she will almost certainly want to tell you about.''

"I see," Longarm replied, knowing the type. "Well, we're planning on going up to Mesa Verde soon. And we'd like to buy some Anasazi artifacts.''

"Oh, you can find them for sale all over town. Skulls. Pots. Flints. Metates. Whatever you need.''

"Who is the biggest dealer in Cortez?" Longarm asked. "You see, we are collectors.''

"Oh, then you'd probably want to go over to the Cortez Museum and talk to its curator and owner, Mr. Laird. He buys and sells some things, but as you probably know, it's illegal to go up there anymore and loot the cliff dwellings. Besides, Richard Wetherill and his family, who discovered most of them cliff dwellings, already took out a bunch of stuff.''

"Are the Wetherills around here now?''

"They've moved south. I understand that Richard is raising cattle and exploring some other ruins, but I don't know for sure. Right now, there's only a couple of scientists excavating up at Mesa Verde.''

"Scientists?''

"That's right. They're excavating at Cliff Palace and some of the lesser-known ruins. You know, digging them up and then trying to preserve and protect them.''

"I see. Have they been up there for quite some time?''

"Oh, yeah. They work for some university. They're real archaeologists and pretty standoffish.''

Longarm nodded with understanding. "How often do they come down to Cortez?"

"As little as possible. They're not real friendly, and even when they come into town they don't stay long. Just long enough to pick up their mail and restock their supplies."

"I understand," Longarm said. "What are their names?"

"Arthur Lucking and John Barker. But you'd better not address them as anything but 'Doctor,' or they get mad and act insulted. I guess they're real smart."

"Are they removing artifacts from Mesa Verde?" Miranda asked, unable to keep quiet any longer.

"Some, I think. We never see what they're doing 'cause they are camped way back on the mesa."

"Do they work with anyone locally?"

"No," the liveryman said, "but I do know that they are supplied by Mountain Packers out of Durango."

Longarm cussed himself for not having that knowledge when he'd been in Durango. If the archaeologists were in on the theft of the artifacts—and he had a hunch that they ought to be his immediate prime suspects—then Mountain Packers would most likely be their way of delivering illegal artifacts from the cliff dwellings.

"Mister, are you and your wife planning a ride up there yourselves, or do you want to hire a professional guide?"

"We hadn't decided."

"Well," the liveryman told them, "I'd recommend a guide who is very familiar with Mesa Verde and its ruins. Someone who can really show you everything and has some knowledge of the cliff dwellings."

"I suppose you just happen to know exactly such a person, right?"

"As a matter of fact, I do! My brother, Matt Horn, is one of the best. He's been going up to Mesa Verde for years and knows every inch of the area. He can tell you lots of stories, and he's a first-class packer, cook, and wrangler."

"How much does he charge?"

"Since you already have horses and that burro for packing, Matt would probably give you a hefty discount."

"He ought to."

"Why don't I send Matt over to meet you at the Concord Hotel this afternoon and you can sit down and talk things over. If it's a match, I'll even give you a discount on keeping your horses at my livery. Don't see how you can beat such a deal as that."

"All right," Longarm said. "But instead of this afternoon, have him come on over about nine o'clock tomorrow morning and we can talk over breakfast. My wife and I are pretty tuckered out from the traveling."

"You came in from the direction of Pueblo, didn't you?"

"That's right."

"You have any trouble with that gang that's been robbing stagecoaches and their passengers?"

"As a matter of fact, we did," Longarm said, not wanting to tell the story and create any interest in or curiosity about himself. "Send Matt over to the hotel at nine and we'll try to get something settled," he said, turning to leave.

"You'll like him!" the liveryman called. "And I'll make sure that he gives you a full tour at a rate better than you could get anywhere else in Cortez!"

Longarm and Miranda walked into the Concord Hotel, and the first thing that happened was that a little old woman no bigger than a minute sized them up and then proclaimed, "My name is *Miss* Jenny McAllister! Who are you?"

Longarm introduced himself and Miranda as Mr. and Mrs. Long.

"We're on our honeymoon," Miranda said, squeezing his arm. "We've come from Denver to see the cliff dwellings up at Mesa Verde."

"Well, now!" Jenny said. "You are in for a real treat! Wait until you see Cliff Palace, Square Tower, and Balcony House! Why, you'll want to move right in yourselves! You see, the ancient ones knew what they were doing when they built their homes up in them sandstone cliffs! Yes, sir, they're out of the wind and snow and most are south-facing, where they get the winter sunshine that would heat their rock houses so that they kept warm even on the coldest nights."

"We're very anxious to see them."

"You got a guide picked out yet? I got a cousin that—"

"We're going to talk to Matt Horn," Longarm said, cutting the woman off.

"Well," Jenny said, frowning, "Matt is a good man and he sure knows the ruins as well as most anyone around. His brother Joe runs the livery. But I hear Matt's a *terrible* cook."

"We don't mind that," Miranda said. "Have you lived in Cortez long?"

"Most of my life," the woman said. "My husband and I bought this hotel from a woman whose husband got drunk and got stabbed to death in a saloon brawl about twelve years ago. Then my husband, he up and died about five years ago, leaving all the damned work to me. I don't mind, though. I can hire Chinamen or whoever I need to help, and sit on the veranda in my rocking chair and watch the world go by."

"Sounds like a good life," Longarm said.

"Oh, it is! I'm looking for a husband, though. One about your age and size, Mr. Long." Jenny winked. "Too bad that you're already taken, or maybe we could have had some good times together."

Longarm chuckled, knowing that he was being teased. "Well," he told the old woman, "if I see any likely prospects, I'll send them your way, Miss McAllister."

"You do that and you and your pretty wife can stay here as long as you like for free!" Jenny strutted behind her registration desk and pulled a key from a board. "I'm givin' you Room Number Five. It has a nice view."

"Much obliged."

"Be a dollar a day for the room, and you get a bath every day whether you need it or not and clean sheets every week. If you want meals here, I have a dining room and my food is as good and as reasonable as you'll find in Cortez. Tonight, we're having corned beef and cabbage with sourdough bread and apple pie for dessert. All you can eat and all the coffee you can drink. Fifty cents each and you won't do better anywhere else."

"That sounds good," Miranda said. "I'm sure that we will be down for supper."

"Good!"

Longarm paid for two nights and took his room key. Number Five had a nice view of the main street. The place was modest but clean, and when a couple of Chinamen arrived with pails of hot water for their bath, Longarm tipped them generously. Being a gentleman, Longarm offered Miranda the first turn in the big copper tub.

No," she said, "you're dirtier than I am, so you go first."

"That tub is big enough for the both of us," Longarm argued. "So why don't we both get in while the water is still nice and hot."

"I like that idea," Miranda said, starting to remove her clothes.

Longarm undressed quickly, and enthusiastically climbed into the tub, groaning with contentment because the water felt so soothing. When Miranda joined him, he could not help himself as he studied her large and luscious breasts and the graceful curve where her slender neck met her pretty shoulders.

"Why are you looking at me like that?" she asked, cocking her head a little to one side.

"You are so beautiful that I was thinking how much I'd like to make love to you."

"In this tub?" Miranda looked at him as if he were crazy.

"That's right."

She giggled. "Could you? I mean, it's not *that* big!"

"Yes, it is," he said, coming over to ease down between her legs. "Have you ever done it in a bathtub?"

"No, and I think it sounds kind of crazy when we have a nice, dry bed just a few feet away."

"I like the novelty of this," Longarm said, rocking his hips forward as he guided his throbbing shaft into her body. "There, I told you it would work."

She hugged his neck and scooted down a little so he could enter her all the way. "Custis, be honest. This could get pretty sloppy, couldn't it?"

"It could and it probably will," he said, kissing her lips as he began to move around and around as if he were stirring a big spoon.

"You won't lose your head and half drown me like male ducks do to female ducks when they screw them on a pond or lake, will you?"

"No, I promise that won't happen." Longarm grinned with pleasure. "After this, you'll want to make love more often in a bathtub."

"I'd make love *anywhere* with you," Miranda said, her own bottom beginning to thrust. "This is nice and warm and . . . different."

Longarm closed his eyes and lost himself in the pleasure of their lovemaking. He took his time, and it was nearly a quarter of an hour before both he and Miranda really got excited and started thumping so hard that they splashed waves of water over the rim of the tub.

"We're going to have a big mess on the floor," Miranda panted, clinging to Longarm as he neared his climax.

"Who gives a damn!"

"Not me," she breathed, fingernails digging into his back as her body began to buck wildly out of control. "Oh, come on, Custis!"

Longarm was more than ready, and when he exploded, he sent great tidal waves of water sloshing onto the floor. Moments later, spent and relaxed, they used what water remained in the copper tub to scrub each other clean with green soap and a washcloth.

"My," Miranda said after toweling dry, looking flushed from the hot water and her passion. "That sort of thing really takes it out of a woman."

"And a man," Longarm said, padding across the wet floor and climbing into their bed. "Why don't we take a nap before we join Jenny McAllister and whoever else will be dining downstairs?"

"Good idea! I'd like that just fine," Miranda said,

yawning. "That trip and all the trouble that we had sort of took its toll on me."

"Me too," Longarm said, drawing her in close to his body and then pulling the covers over them both.

"I thought you'd want to start your investigation almost the moment we arrived," Miranda whispered as he started to drift into a heavy sleep.

"Naw, I'll go out this evening and hang around the saloons and see what I can find out."

"Do you think that Mountain Packers and those two archaeologists are behind the thefts?"

"I don't know," Longarm admitted. "The last thing I want to do is to make any snap judgments. They probably are legitimate scientists, but on the other hand, that sure would be a great cover for robbing Indian graves."

"What about taking a guide with us up to Mesa Verde?"

"What about it?" Longarm asked, finding it difficult to stay awake.

"Well, we don't want to put anyone else's life in danger, so I just thought that—"

"We need a guide if we're to look legitimate," Longarm said. "Can we please talk about this later?"

"Just like a man," she said. "Love a woman, then either go away or go to sleep."

"You talk way too damn much some of the time," he said with a lazy smile.

They slept for four hours. It was sundown when they climbed out of bed and got dressed. "It's nearly seven o'clock," Longarm said. "Did Jenny McAllister say what time she put food on her dining room table?"

"No," Miranda answered, "but I expect that it has already come and gone."

"I'm not that crazy about corned beef and cabbage

anyway," he admitted. "I saw several cafes in town, and this is cattle country. I can't imagine that we can't order a pretty good steak with potatoes and all the rest."

"I agree." Miranda finished dressing and studied herself in the mirror. "You sure know how to mess up a woman's hair."

"You just happen to be the kind of woman that any healthy man would want to mess up a little," he replied. "I'm ready when you are."

"Well!" Jenny McAllister called across the lobby when they came downstairs. "It's a good thing that you *finally* got out of bed. My other guests have already eaten and departed, but I saved you plenty of corned beef and cabbage. Come on into the dining room and I'll fix you both up."

Longarm started to tell the woman that she needn't go to all the trouble, but Miranda shook her head, letting him know that their fate was sealed and that they should just be gracious and forget about a steak dinner.

"Sit down! Sit down!" Jenny McAllister ordered, "and we will have hot food on your plates in a jiffy!"

The same two grinning Chinamen who had lugged pails of hot bathwater up to their room served them supper, and Longarm had to admit that this was as good as corned beef and cabbage ever got. He was famished, and even ordered seconds. Miranda had no trouble doing the same.

"Well, then," Jenny said, "I can see that lovemaking *still* generates a fantastic appetite!"

Miranda blushed, but Longarm laughed out loud, then asked, "Are you always so plainspoken, Miss McAllister?"

"Please call me Jenny. And yes, I am. Always have been and always will be. I say whatever is on my mind,

107

and that keeps my mind from becoming secretive or vulgar."

"Oh, really?" Miranda asked.

"That's right," the older woman replied. "I just hate secretive people. I have a theory that if everyone was a whole lot more honest with themselves and with all others, this would be a far, far better world."

"I can't argue with that," Miranda said. "Have you been up to Mesa Verde many times?"

"Oh, heavens, yes! My late husband Willard loved the ruins, and we'd go up for a month every summer. It's cooler up there than it is down here in Cortez, and we would have a wonderful time camping and exploring."

"We are interested in Anasazi artifacts," Longarm said. "But I understand that they are now under federal protection."

"That's right," Jenny told them. "But that legislation was too little and too late. The Wetherills already freighted out piles of valuable artifacts. There was even a damned foreigner who had a bunch of things sent to Europe! He was a baron or something and a real dandy. When everyone learned that he was taking Indian bones, pots, and the like to Sweden, they had a fit and raised such an uproar that the baron had to practically flee for his life."

"What do you know about the two archaeologists that are working up on the mesa-top right now?"

"Not much," Jenny said, frowning with clear disapproval. "They are really stuck-up. I've tried to engage them in conversation several times, but they brushed me off as if I were an insect. I don't like either one of them! And I don't like the fact that they are up there doing

God only knows what. Why, they could be *destroying* artifacts left and right!''

"Or selling them for profit," Longarm said with an innocent shrug of his shoulders.

Their hotel keeper blinked with surprise, then asked, "Why did you say that?"

"Well, couldn't they be?" Longarm asked with a disarming smile. "I mean, has *anyone* seen their credentials?"

"No," Jenny said, "I suppose not. But when they first arrived, I understand they had some official papers. I think they showed them to a few people just to establish their identities. And besides, they are obviously scientists."

"How do you know that?" Miranda asked.

"People who have visited their camp have seen their books and sketches. Their measuring and excavation devices and tools. They are far more sophisticated than the Wetherills or anyone else who has been up there working."

"I see," Longarm said, not seeing at all.

To his way of thinking, the pair could be legitimate scientists working for a very illegitimate consortium of thieves. Scientists, after all, were only human beings like everyone else. They liked money too. They could easily be scientists who had been corrupted by ill-gained gains.

They talked for almost an hour after the meal, and Longarm pretty much learned all that he could learn about Mesa Verde and the two supposed archaeologists from Jenny McAllister. After that, they excused themselves and soon retired upstairs to their room.

"I'll go out and see what I can learn in the saloons," Longarm said.

"Be very careful."

"I've nothing to worry about," Longarm assured her. "I'm just a fella who is lucky enough to have married a beautiful woman who also enjoys the outdoors and ancient Indian history. That's it."

"What if someone from your past recognizes you and remembers that you are a United States marshal?"

"That is a possibility," Longarm admitted. "But then again, it will be dim in those saloons, and I mostly keep my mouth shut and my hat pulled down low. Given my size, most folks just kind of give me a wide berth."

"I see." Miranda kissed his mouth. "Please don't stay out too late. I'll be waiting for you."

"Go to sleep, Miranda. I'll wake you up when I return."

"Promise?"

"Yes, I promise."

"All right then. And I suppose that you'll want to climb onto me and do it again, huh?"

"Probably. Is that all right?"

"I'd be disappointed and worried if you didn't," she told him as she began to undress and get ready for bed.

Longarm knew that if he stayed and watched, he would start undressing too. So he kissed Miranda good night and went out on the town to see if he could find out any more about the archaeologists and the ancient Indian ruins.

Chapter 10

Longarm went out that evening expecting that he would not be gone more than an hour or two. After all, there were only three saloons in all of Cortez, and none of them could be that crowded. Still, as he leisurely strolled down the boardwalk, he was surprised that there were so many cowboys and other workingmen moving about.

"What day is it?" he asked a middle-aged and smallish cowboy who was talking to a large, bib-wearing miner.

"Why, it's Saturday and payday for most of us," the cowboy said. "You new in town?"

"I am," Longarm replied, pulling out and lighting a cheroot. "I'm from Denver."

"You lookin' for work?" the miner asked. " 'Cause you're big enough that you wouldn't have any trouble finding it at one of the mines."

"No," Longarm said, "I'm here on my honeymoon. My wife and I have always wanted to see the Mesa Verde cliff dwellings, and that's why we came to Cortez."

"Damn," the cowboy said, shaking his head, "if I was just married, the *last* place on this green earth that I'd want to take my bride would be up there among all them spooks. What you want to do that for? Nothin' but old bones and pots and maybe some Indian ghosts up in that country."

"Well," Longarm said without attempting to hide his amusement at this evaluation, "we collect old Indian artifacts and have an interest in those kinds of things."

"That's sure hard to figure," the miner said, his chin jutting out a moment before he dragged a pint of whiskey out of his bib overalls. "Stranger, do you know what my personal theory is about them cliff dwellings and all them dusty old ruins and the dumb Indians who built 'em?"

"No," Longarm answered, "but I have a feeling that I'm about to learn it."

The miner cleared his throat and loudly pronounced, "A dead Injun . . . is a dead Injun . . . is a dead Injun."

"Well," Longarm said, unable to hide his sarcasm, "that certainly is profound."

"Huh?"

"Never mind." Longarm started to push past the miner, but the man grabbed his arm.

"Hey," the miner said, "was you just makin' fun of me?"

"Nope."

"Sure you was! I know when some uppity sumbitch is tweakin' my nose."

"Getting it 'tweaked' is better than getting it busted," Longarm said with a cold smile. "Wouldn't you agree?"

The miner was a little drunk, but the cowboy, being

more sober, had more sense. "Come on, Clem. Let's go inside and have us another round."

"Excellent advice," Longarm said as he pulled his arm free and started to go inside himself.

But the miner tried to grab Longarm again and, this time, bash him in the side of the face. Longarm brought his right fist up in a short, powerful arc that connected against the side of the miner's jaw and dropped him to the sidewalk.

"Hey!" the cowboy shouted, jumping back and raising his open hands. "I ain't interested in trying to finish what this fool tried to start."

Longarm rubbed his knuckles and said, "Why don't you drag him into an alley where the fool can sleep it off. Then come on inside and I'll buy you a beer to show that I've no hard feelings."

"Why, that would be real nice of you, mister!" the cowboy said, grinning broadly. "It sure would!"

Longarm went into the saloon. The place was packed with boisterous workingmen, and the floor was covered with sawdust. There was a piano player, but no one could hear his music because of the shouting and laughter. The bar itself was nothing but a long, flat plank laid across whiskey barrels. Not a novel creation in this part of the country by any means.

"What will it be?" the bartender asked as Longarm shouldered between some laughing men and made himself a little room.

"Couple of beers."

"Comin' up!"

The beers came just as the cowboy returned, slightly out of breath. "Name is Dudley," he said. "What's yours?"

"Custis. Have you lived in these parts very long?"

"About ten years now. I work for the Cross X Ranch. It's a good outfit and they pay on a regular basis, most of the time."

Longarm raised his glass in salute, and Dudley did the same. After they had a long swallow, Longarm said, "You ever work for an outfit called Mountain Packers?"

"Nope. But I've heard about 'em. They operate out of Durango and pack in supplies for the tourists and other people going up to Mesa Verde. Why do you ask?"

"Oh," Longarm said, "I was just curious. Do they take supplies in on wagons or—"

"On pack animals," Dudley answered. "There's no road up to the mesa-top. It's a pretty steep climb and rugged."

"I see."

"But you can find local people here that will take you and your bride up to Mesa Verde."

"I think I'm going to use a man named Matt Horn."

"Matt is one of the best around and he'll take care of you," Dudley said, nodding with approval.

"We're hoping to find some old Indian pottery, bones, or like that as souvenirs."

"They passed a law against doing that."

"So I've heard."

"If you want some *good* stuff, you ought to see Mr. Laird. He owns the museum and I hear that he sells things on the side. They're not cheap, though. I know a fella that bought an Anasazi pot that was all in one piece, and he paid a fortune for the damned thing. Over fifty dollars!"

"Boy," Longarm said, "that is high. Where does this Mr. Laird get his stuff?"

"I expect that he bought a lot of it from the Wetherills

114

when they were hauling it out in the early years. But every time I've been in that museum, there's new stuff, so he just might have a new supplier.''

"Maybe he's making fake pottery," Longarm offered.

"Nope. It's real. Them two scientists working up there always stop in at the museum, and they say that it's all real stuff. Hell, they ought to know, don't you think?''

"Yes, I do," Longarm said. "But I wonder if someone *else* is excavating up there that no one knows about.''

"That's possible. It's also possible that some rancher has found an excavation site, an old Indian burial or building ground, and is digging it up on his own land.''

"I see. I've also heard that there have been killings and shootings over the artifacts.''

Dudley eyed Longarm closely. "You've heard quite a bit for a total stranger.''

"I like to know what I'm getting into," Longarm said with a shrug. "After all, a man wouldn't want to take his wife up someplace where their might be danger.''

"That's true enough. And there have been a couple of people shot up on the mesa as well as out near the Hovenweep ruins farther west. Some say there is a ring of thieves that work the cliff dwellings, and that is why several people have disappeared. But most of us think they were killed by the Utes, who consider Mesa Verde and them ruins as sacred ground.''

"Has anyone spoken to the Utes?''

"Naw. Most of them have been wiped out, and what is left is just small bands here and there. They keep on the move, but I expect that they're the real killers.''

"Do you know a Miss Candice Mason?''

"Sure! Candice owns the Bull's Eye Ranch about ten

miles west of here not far from Hovenweep, where some of the trouble has been going on. Miss Mason's mother died when she was just a kid, and her father and brother were murdered about two years ago when they were bringing some cattle money back from Utah. Candice has several hundred head of cattle and some pretty good grazing land. She don't like or trust men. No one can work for her for very long. She's got skin thicker than rawhide, but she's a handsome gal.''

"She live alone?''

"Naw, she's got a small crew of old geezers that couldn't find work on any other spread and probably ought to be riding rocking chairs. She's got some of the biggest, most ferocious damned dogs that you ever seen. And she can shoot the eye out of a gawddamn mosquito at a hundred yards.''

"She sounds like a real hellion.''

"You got that right. Because she's pretty and pretty women are as scarce as hen's teeth in these parts, she has had a lot of young bucks that have tried to soften up her heart. But she ain't got a heart. Just a stone where her heart ought to be, and since her father and brother were murdered, she's turned meaner than a rattlesnake.''

"I see.'' Longarm frowned. It was now obvious that his boss, Billy Vail, hadn't told him half the story about Candice Mason.

"You want another beer?'' the cowboy asked, rifling his pockets but coming up empty.

"No,'' Longarm said, "but I'll buy you another before I leave.''

"Why, you are a gentleman of the highest order!'' Dudley exclaimed.

Longarm bought the cowboy another beer, knowing he'd gained some very valuable information but that

Dudley probably couldn't tell him anything else of value. It was time to go visit another saloon.

The Red Goose Saloon was loud and tough. Most of the customers were drunk, and the place didn't serve anything but bad whiskey at a nickel a shot. Longarm had one shot and damn near doubled over in pain.

"Damn!" he complained, making a face. "What's in this crap! Rat poison?"

"Naw," the bartender said with a comforting grin. "But the boys that come in here want to get drunk fast, and so we have a *special* brew made for just that purpose. You drink three shots and you're feeling like you can whip the world. You drink five shots and you'll think that you *are* the world. Seven shots will put you to sleep for two days, and ten will probably kill you. I dunno because no one has ever got past eight."

"Well," Longarm said, "I sure won't be the first. I'm new in town and headed up to Mesa Verde. Have you been up there before?"

"A time or two," the bartender said. "But to be honest with you, it gives me the creeps."

"What about *you*?" Longarm asked the man at his right elbow.

"You ever been up there?"

The man just stared at him with unfocused eyes. When he tried to say something, his words made no sense at all. Longarm turned to the man on his left, who at least seemed conscious.

"You ever been up to Mesa Verde and seen the old Indian cliff dwellings?"

"Sure! A couple of times. Gawdamm interesting, if you ask me."

"Well," Longarm said, playing the tourist, "my wife and I are going up there on our honeymoon."

117

"Huh?"

"Our honeymoon."

"You're goin' up to them old Indian ruins on your *honeymoon*?"

"Yeah."

"Jaysus," the man said, shaking his head, "that's sure not very romantic!"

Longarm had the feeling that this man wasn't going to do anything but get argumentative, so he ordered another of the poison whiskeys and moved on down the bar, looking to talk to a few more people in the hope that someone could tell him a little more about the grave robbers who were supposed to be over at Four Corners, or about Mr. Laird or Mountain Packers.

He did find several more people who knew about those things and were willing to share their knowledge for the price of a drink or two. But by midnight, Longarm figured that he was about played out, and he was ready to go back to the Concord Hotel, climb into bed with Miranda, and go to sleep. Longarm was bone-weary, and he sure hoped that Miranda would forgive him for just wanting to sleep.

"Howdy," a big, smiling man said as Longarm stepped out of the saloon. "I understand that you are looking for a guide to take you and your wife up to Mesa Verde."

Longarm nodded. The man was his size and age, big in the shoulders and heavy in the chest. "That's right," he answered, "but I have chosen Matt Horn."

"I'm better than Horn and I won't charge you as much. What is he asking?"

"I don't know," Longarm said. "We haven't talked yet."

"Why don't you forget about Horn," the man said.

"You won't find a better guide than me."

"I like a man with confidence, but I think I'll talk to Horn anyway. However, if we can't come to terms, I'd be happy to talk to you. What is your name?"

"John. Maybe I'll see you tomorrow."

Longarm didn't think so. He was a pretty good judge of character, and he didn't like this man's challenging and rather arrogant attitude. So he turned and started across the street toward the Concord Hotel. The next thing he knew, he heard the blast of a rifle and felt a slug whip past his cheek. Longarm threw himself down, rolled, and came up with his gun in his hand. He looked for a target, but there was none. The street was empty. The big man named John had vanished, but then Longarm wasn't a bit sure that he had been the one that had opened fire. He was even less sure when a wooden shingle from a rooftop across the street fell to the sidewalk.

Longarm dashed across the street and ran down the dark corridor between the buildings, then skidded to a halt in a dark alley. He heard the pounding of boots, and took off after them, but crashed blindly into an old rain barrel, knocking it over and landing in mud.

"Dammit!" he raged, scrambling to his feet, then groping his way back out onto the main street. "Dammit anyway!"

When he got back to his hotel room Longarm knew that he was filthy, and not wanting to get the bed or Miranda dirty, he returned to the lobby and asked a sleepy night clerk to send up some hot bathwater.

"The Chinamen have gone for the night and I'm afraid that bath time is over. However, I will personally deliver you a couple of pails of room-temperature water."

"Just give them to me now."

"What happened?" the clerk asked. "How did you—"

"Don't even ask."

"I heard gunfire. Was someone killed?"

"Almost."

Longarm took the water upstairs and washed by candlelight. Then he climbed into bed. Miranda was sound asleep, and although he was exhausted, it took him a good hour to fall asleep. Mostly because he was wondering who in the deuce had tried to ambush and kill him . . . and why?

Someone has recognized me and knows that I'm a federal marshal. Someone who wants me dead.

There could be no other possible explanation, and that meant that he had lost the element of surprise. That was bad. Very bad indeed.

Chapter 11

"Custis, what happened to your clothes?" Miranda asked him the following morning when they awakened. "Did you get drunk and fall over into a horse's watering trough?"

"Don't be ridiculous."

"Well, then, did you try to drink a pail of beer?"

Longarm saw no point in telling Miranda that he had nearly been ambushed. It would only upset her for no good reason. So he just laughed and kissed her, saying, "There are some pretty wild saloons in this town."

"What did you find out?"

He told her everything he had learned, even about Candice Mason and the feeling by most locals that the killings on Mesa Verde had been committed by renegade Ute Indians.

"Do you believe that?" Miranda asked him.

"I don't know," Longarm admitted. "It's possible. I know that Indian peoples are very touchy about their ancestors and their old burial grounds—just as we would be if someone tried to dig up our grandfather or grandmother. So, it could be that the Utes are behind the killings, but I'd say that the odds are definitely against that."

"Why?"

"From what I could learn, the bodies were never found. If you were trying to warn the whites to stay out of your ancestors' homes and burial grounds, wouldn't you leave the bodies for everyone to see? And another thing, Indians aren't generally that devious. They are expert at stealing horses, but when it comes to killing, generally they are pretty straightforward."

"So what do we do now?"

"Well," Longarm said, "we need to talk to Matt Horn about guiding us up to the ruins so I can meet those archaeologists and try and figure out if they are legitimate or if their work is just a cover for the grave robbers. So let's get dressed and get busy."

They dressed and went downstairs for the breakfast meeting Matt Horn. The man was in his early thirties, handsome and rugged-looking, with big hands, a lantern jaw, and penetrating blue eyes. Longarm liked and trusted him immediately, and they quickly came to terms about their trip up to the Mesa Verde ruins.

"It's a two-day ride each way," Matt told them. "I mean, you could make it in one day, but it would be rough. My brother says that you have two good horses and a burro."

"That's right."

"Fine with me," Matt said. "I'll pack everything we need on my own animals and we can leave whenever you say."

"How about we go on Tuesday," Longarm told him. "I've some matters that I want to attend to."

"That suits me just fine," Matt said. "I heard a rumor

that you were involved in some kind of shooting last night. Is that true?''

Miranda's eyes widened. "Custis? Is that true?''

"I guess I should have told you," Longarm said. "But yes, someone did take a shot at me.''

"Who would do a thing like that?'' Matt asked.

"I have no idea," Longarm replied, avoiding Miranda's troubled gaze. "But the most likely explanation is that it was a case of mistaken identity. Either that, or some drunk shooting off a stray bullet that happened to come in my general direction.''

"Boy," Matt said, shaking his head, "I don't know what this country is coming to these days.''

After Matt left, Miranda said, "Why didn't you tell me that someone took a shot at you last night?''

"I didn't want you to worry.''

Her eyes flashed with anger. "If someone took a shot at *me*, don't you think that I'd tell *you*?''

"That would be altogether different," Longarm said. "And besides, maybe it *was* just a stray bullet.''

"You don't believe that and neither do I," Miranda told him. "Someone has recognized you, and maybe they've even heard that you've been asking questions about Mesa Verde and the Anasazi artifacts.''

"All right," Longarm said, "I think that is the most likely explanation for what happened last night, but it is by no means the only one. For example, that bullet might have come from someone who holds a grudge against me for something I've done to them in the past.''

"I see. You probably have made plenty of enemies over the years, haven't you.''

"Yes, I have. Miranda, let's go to the local museum and see what we can find out from Mr. Laird.''

"All right.''

They got their directions on the street, and the museum was easy to find. They sat under a cottonwood tree for a half hour until a man in a gray, pin-striped suit and a black bowler appeared and began to unlock the front door. Longarm judged Laird to be in his early sixties and fairly well-to-do by the look of his clothes.

"Mr. Laird?"

The man turned. "Yes?"

"My name is Custis and this is my wife Miranda. We are quite interested in Anasazi history and looking forward to visiting your museum this morning."

"Well," Laird said with an affable smile, "it's not all *that* much of a collection, but I am adding to it steadily. The charge is fifty cents each, and I'll be available to answer any and all questions pertaining to the cliff dwellers who lived at Mesa Verde."

"Thank you," Longarm said, ushering Miranda inside to see displays of pottery and stone relics, including ax heads and metates used for grinding corn. There were also many photographs and drawings of the cliff dwellings, as well as placards that explained the Anasazi story.

"This is wonderful!" Miranda exclaimed as she moved about, reading and studying the artifacts.

Longarm also found the displays fascinating. He put off questioning Laird until he had studied everything, and then he went to the back of the room, where the museum curator was using a very fine dental pick and some paintbrushes to clean the orifices in an old Indian skull.

"That looks like painstaking work," Longarm said.

Laird glanced up at him. "Yes, it is, but well worth the effort."

"I wonder what killed that man whose skull you are holding."

"Well," Laird said, "it could be most anything. I'm not a professional archaeologist, but I can tell you a few things about this individual. He was probably a man, because the bone is thicker than that of a female skull. And judging from the teeth, he was quite old. The teeth are badly worn, and you can even see that several had abscessed away jawbone. Most of the cliff-dwelling peoples ate corn that they harvested on the mesa-top. It was their primary food, and after it was ground up on the metate, there were so many rock particles in their food that their teeth were ground away at what we think was a relatively young age."

"I see." Longarm leaned over and studied the skull. "And when a man gets bad teeth, he can't eat very well."

"That's right, and that would have been the beginning of the end for a cliff dweller. Stop eating and you lose weight and strength, both of which would have been very necessary for a long and difficult winter survival."

"Where do you get all of these artifacts?" Longarm asked with a smile.

"Oh, here and there. The Wetherill family excavated a great deal of them and either gave them to friends or sold them off for practically nothing until they realized how valuable they were to serious collectors such as myself. The Wetherills are gone now, and many of the people that bought or had these artifacts given to them have either gotten bored with them or have, for one reason or another, decided to sell because they would rather have cash than Anasazi artifacts."

"I see. Where did you get *this* particular skull?"

For the first time, Longarm saw a hint of irritation

cross Laird's face, and it came out in his voice when he said, "I bought it from a local."

"Would you be willing to sell a few things to my wife and myself?"

"Perhaps," Laird said. "Some things, but not others."

"What about that skull?"

"You'd want to buy this?"

"Maybe."

"How odd," Laird said. "I sell pottery and even spearheads and other artifacts, but very few are interested in buying a complete skull."

"I would be," Longarm said. "What is it worth?"

"This skull is in excellent condition, and it will be quite valuable when I have cleaned it up properly. I'd say that it is worth at least three hundred dollars, perhaps more."

"I don't have anywhere near that much money to spend. Oh, I mean, I do, but not on a single artifact."

"Of course," Laird said, managing a tolerant smile. "Now, if you have no other questions . . ."

"I have a few," Miranda said. "Why did the cliff dwellers abandon Mesa Verde?"

"That is the *great* question," Laird replied. "The one that everyone asks, but which no one can really answer. Some believe that the cliff dwellers were destroyed by enemies and taken away into slavery. Others say no, disease killed off their civilization. I say that it could have been a change in the climate. Perhaps a prolonged drought that made it impossible to sustain their farming."

"How would anyone begin to prove those theories?" Miranda asked.

"I can't answer that. There are two excellent archae-

126

ologists up on the mesa right now, a Dr. Barker and a Dr. Lucking. They are on the faculty at Harvard, and have been sent out here to work on excavations and research.''

"Harvard, huh?" Longarm said.

"Yes. They are *excellent* scientists, and far more knowledgeable than I am about ancient civilizations.''

"Do you buy artifacts that they excavate?" Longarm asked.

"No, of course not!" Laird did not even attempt to hide his irritation at this question. "I've already told you where I get my collection. From locals and from what I actually purchased or else found for myself at Mesa Verde.''

"I was only curious because my wife and I were sort of hoping to find a few things for ourselves. It would be more fun than *buying* them.''

"I understand that. But the main cliff dwellings have all been thoroughly examined and excavated. You see, most of the artifacts found in them were buried in their trash piles.''

"Is that a fact?" Longarm asked.

"It is," Laird replied. "This skull and some of its body bones which I have in the storeroom were excavated from a trash heap in the very back of Cliff Palace.''

"They buried their dead in with their trash?" Miranda asked, looking appalled.

"Only in the wintertime when the ground up on the mesa was frozen and burial anywhere else would have been impossible," Laird explained. "We are very sure that was the reason why we find skeletons in their trash heaps. And because those trash heaps were often located very far back under the lip of the limestone caverns, the skeletons never were subject to the elements. That is why they are in such remarkably good condition."

"Isn't that something," Longarm said, shaking his head as if in wonder.

"Yes, it is," Laird agreed. "And we also find buried dogs and many turkey bones."

"Those people raised turkeys?"

"Oh, yes!" Laird came to his feet and went out into his displayed collection, beckoning Longarm and Miranda to follow and examine a ratty-looking robe.

"This is an ancient robe of the kind that we think were quite typical," Laird said, his long, slender fingers stroking the robe's fur. "As you can plainly see, the robe is made of woven strips of leather and turkey feathers. It would have been very, very warm in the winter."

"Amazing," Miranda said, stroking the robe. "It must have taken a great deal of time, effort, and patience for their women to have made these robes."

"Exactly so!" Laird agreed. "But their lives would have depended upon keeping warm during the wintertime."

"Didn't they keep big fires going in the caves?" Longarm asked.

"Oh, certainly! You can see the smoke stains and smudge all over the roofs of those cliff caverns, but the heat would have risen, and I doubt it would have offered any warmth at all to a person who was not sitting directly beside the fire. You see, the roofs are quite high, and since we all know that heat rises, it would have dissipated quickly."

"You sound extremely knowledgeable about the cliff dwellers yourself," Longarm said.

"I have made them a lifetime study," Laird admitted. "And although I do not have a formal academic background in archaeology or anthropology, I daresay that I am quite a recognized expert on the Anasazi and that the two scientists currently working up there depend on me for the answers to certain mysteries.''

''I'm sure that they do,'' Longarm said. Then, turning to Miranda. ''We had better go now and leave this man to his work, my dear.''

''Oh, no,'' Laird protested. ''Stay as long as you wish and ask whatever questions you want. I may not be able to answer them, but I'll try.''

''You're very kind,'' Miranda said sweetly.

Laird actually blushed.

Longarm took Miranda's arm and steered her toward the doorway, saying, ''We'll probably be back.''

''Good!''

When they were outside and walking back toward the hotel, Miranda said, ''Why were you in such a big hurry to leave that museum? There were so many things that I didn't have time to see or questions that you never gave me a chance to ask.''

''Good,'' Longarm told her, ''because I want to come back several times without arousing the man's suspicion. Did you notice how defensive he became when I asked him about the source of his collection?''

''No.''

''Well,'' Longarm said, ''he became *very* defensive and, I thought, very vague.''

''Vague? I heard him tell you that he bought most of his collection from locals who needed money.''

''Sure, but I had the feeling that he didn't want to mention any names. Perhaps while I am gone tomorrow, you could ask around about who is selling to the man.''

''Gone?'' Miranda stopped cold in her tracks. ''Where are you going without me?''

"I want to visit the person who alerted my department about the possibility of thefts," Longarm answered. "She has a ranch a few miles east."

"Fine," Miranda said. "We can both ride out there."

"I'd rather that you didn't," Longarm said. "And besides, it will be a long ride up to Mesa Verde and it might do you well to rest up for it."

"I suppose that is true."

Longarm took her arm and started back to the hotel. Later, he would go to the telegraph office and send a message to Billy Vail, asking him to check the references of Drs. Lucking and Barker with Harvard University. If they really were on the Harvard faculty, he could probably eliminate them from suspicion. Probably, but not completely. However, if Harvard replied that they had never heard of either man, then it was almost certain that they were impostors and involved in the gang that was looting Indian artifacts.

"I liked Mr. Laird," Miranda said. "You may be suspicious of him, but I'm not. I think he was quite honest with us."

"Maybe," Longarm said. "Maybe."

Chapter 12

The next morning Longarm had ridden less than a mile out of Cortez when he saw a young woman and two old cowboys coming into view. The woman was riding a spunky sorrel mare, while the two hands were seated in a rickety buckboard wagon. She had long blond hair and blue eyes, and hid her figure well with an old leather jacket that was about three sizes too large. Longarm wondered if he'd just gotten lucky.

"Miss Mason?" he asked when he drew up alongside the woman and her buckboard. "Miss Candice Mason?"

"That's right," she said, eyeing him suspiciously, "and who the hell are you?"

"I'm a friend," Longarm said, not wanting to let the two older cowboys know that he was a lawman.

"No, you're not. You're a stranger and you are blocking the road. Get out of our way."

One of her cowboys reached for a buggy whip, but Longarm said, "All right, Miss Mason, I work for United States Marshal Billy Vail, who sent me here to see if I could help sort out your troubles. I was just coming out to see you."

Candice studied him closely. "Have you got a badge or anything to prove what you say?"

"Sure," Longarm said, reaching inside his coat pocket, "but I'm traveling as a tourist and I'd like to keep my real identity a secret."

"We can do that," the driver of the buckboard said. "No problem."

"Good." Longarm showed them all his badge. "Now, Miss Mason, I'd appreciate it if we could have a private conversation."

"Anything you have to say to me you can say to my men," Candice told him. "I trust them with my life."

"All right. I take it that you are going into Cortez, probably for supplies?"

"That's correct."

"Then I'll ride along with you," Longarm decided. "We have plenty to talk about."

"Fine," Candice told him. "I just wish that Billy would have sent two or three lawmen instead of one."

"If I need help," Longarm told her, "I can always send for reinforcements."

"It took you a damn long time to get here," Candice argued, "so what makes you think that reinforcements could save your bacon if you get in a fix?"

"Let that be *my* worry," Longarm replied as he reined in next to the woman. "Why don't you tell me everything that you know about this gang of grave robbers."

Candice was quiet for a moment as she composed her thoughts. In the meantime, Longarm couldn't help but stare because she really was a beautiful woman, although there was a hardness in her he found disturbing. Maybe it came from losing both her mother and father and from the heavy ranching responsibilities she had inherited. But whatever the reason, it was definitely present.

"Lawman, what's your name?"

"Custis."

"Well, Custis," Candice began, "what we have going on in this part of the state is a sophisticated bunch of grave robbers. We're not dealing with just a couple of fellas with picks and shovels out to make a few extra bucks. No, sir! We have thievery on a grand scale."

"I've been asking a lot of questions since I left Denver," Longarm said, "and I know about those scientists up at Mesa Verde. Do you believe they are part of the gang?"

"Sure! They're the ones that are doing the actual looting under the guise of science. But they aren't *real* archaeologists."

"How do you know that?"

"I just know," Candice said. "And I've spied on them enough to learn that they are sending most of their stolen artifacts back to Durango on the pack animals that drop off their supplies."

"Do those pack animals belong to an outfit called Mountain Packers?"

Candice actually smiled. "So, you *have* been asking some questions! And guess who owns Mountain Packers."

"Mr. Laird?"

"Bravo!" Candice exclaimed. "But I am sure Laird has a partner in Durango. Someone who packs and routes the stolen artifacts to an international market."

"What makes you think that?"

"It only makes sense that Laird would have a partner," Candice said, shrugging her shoulders. "Of course, he buys and sells artifacts through his museum, but not nearly enough to make it profitable for an organized gang of thieves.''

"Have you ever followed Laird to Durango just to see who he might be dealing with?''

"No," Candice said, "I'm much too busy trying to raise cattle and keep my ranch going. But I don't think it would be hard for a man like yourself to do that.''

"This is all just conjecture, of course," Longarm said. "We need some proof that the two scientists are fakes and that Laird is the go-between for a gang transporting and selling the treasures.''

"Why don't you telegraph someone back East and have them check up on Barker and Lucking? I'm sure that Harvard has never heard of either man.''

"As a matter of fact," Longarm said, "I sent a telegram off just before I left Cortez asking Billy Vail to do that very thing.''

"How is he?''

"Billy is fine. He sends his regards.''

"I never knew him very well, but my parents said that he once helped them out of some kind of bad fix.''

"Billy was a fine lawman during the years he was in the field," Longarm told her. "It's a shame that he settled for a desk job, but he seems happy and has a nice family.''

"Yeah," Candice said, "I guess the life you lead wouldn't be very good for a marriage or family, huh?''

"That's right," Longarm agreed. "It wouldn't.''

She studied him with such frankness that Longarm felt a little uncomfortable. "Maybe you should find a new line of work, Custis.''

"Such as?''

"Do you know anything about cowboying or cattle ranching?''

"Nope. The only thing I know about cattle is that they taste good when they've been cut up and cooked medium rare."

Candice laughed. "At least you are honest. But you're still young enough to learn ranching."

Longarm decided that the conversation was getting way out of hand. "I'm married," he lied. "My wife is waiting for me at the Concord Hotel. A fella named Matt Horn is taking us up to Mesa Verde tomorrow."

"You brought your *wife*?"

Candice looked appalled. Longarm tried to ignore that, and added, "Miranda is very interested in Anasazi artifacts, and she has always wanted to see the cliff dwellings."

"That may be," Candice said, "but it seems a little foolish to me to have her around when you are trying to find a gang of thieves who are probably also killers. I'd have thought that a man with your obvious experience would have known better than to bring along his wife."

"Look," Longarm said, "why don't we just pretend that we don't even know each other. I'll ride on ahead and you and your buckboard can come in later. Tomorrow, I'll let Mr. Horn take my wife and me up to Mesa Verde and I'll do my best to find out what is *really* going on there."

"That's fine with me," Candice said, "just as long as we agree that you'll keep me posted on what you find and what you intend to do about it."

"I'll keep you posted," he promised.

"All right, but I ought to warn you that this gang isn't stupid. If you start asking questions, they're bound to become suspicious, and then they'll put a bullet through your brisket."

Longarm tipped his hat to the ranch woman. "Thanks for the warning," he said a moment before he set his horse into an easy lope heading back to Cortez.

He had unsaddled his horse and was headed for the hotel when Candice and her two old cowpunchers arrived in town. Longarm guessed he was the only man in Cortez who did not stare at the attractive young woman. Even wearing an old leather coat and with most of her blond hair bunched up under a soiled Stetson, Candice was a beauty. She had long legs, and rode her horse as if she had been born in the saddle.

"Ain't she something, though?" a man standing beside Longarm said with unconcealed admiration. "Too bad she's a damned man-hater."

"Yeah," Longarm replied before he wheeled around and went up to his hotel room.

"I didn't expect you back so soon," Miranda said when he entered their room. "I had the impression that you would be gone all day."

"I would have been," he said, "but I met the people I wanted to see coming into town for supplies."

"Did you learn anything new?"

"Not much," he said. "But I expect that we'll know quite a lot more after visiting Mesa Verde and talking to those two Harvard archaeologists."

"Are you hungry?" she asked.

"Famished," he said, "for *you*."

Miranda giggled and came into his arms. Longarm carried her to their bed and they made love until sunset, then went out to get some food to eat.

They went to bed right after dinner, and the next morning they were up quite early. According to their arrangement with Matt Horn, they were simply to pack their clothes and come over to the livery where he would be waiting to take them up to Mesa Verde.

"It's chilly out this morning," Miranda said as they moved across the nearly deserted street toward the livery.

"Yes, and imagine what it will be like up on the mesa," Longarm said. "I have a feeling that we should have made this trip a few months earlier."

When they reached the livery, they were surprised to find that it was dark and seemingly empty.

"This is odd," Longarm said. "I had expected Matt and his brother to be up and about. Matt said that it was a two-day ride up to the cliff dwellings, and I can't imagine why he wouldn't be here."

"Me neither," Miranda said. "So what shall we do?"

"I'll find a lantern," Longarm said, striking a match. "And then we'll go ahead and saddle the horses and do whatever we can to ready ourselves for the trip. Maybe Matt and his brother just overslept."

Longarm held the match up and entered the livery barn. He heard a horse nicker anxiously, and then he saw a lantern hanging from a nail affixed to a thick post. Lighting the lantern, he adjusted the wick and removed it from its place. He'd just turned around to tell Miranda to come inside when something out of the ordinary caught his eye.

"Custis?"

"Miranda, just stay where you are for a minute," he called, moving forward toward a pair of boots that were barely sticking out from under the gate of a nearby stall. "I'll be right with you."

The boots were attached to the body of Matt Horn. The guide's throat had been cut from ear to ear, and blood covered the straw upon which he rested.

"Holy Moses," Longarm whispered before he knelt beside the body and did a quick inventory.

Horn's pockets had been rifled, and there was nothing of value on his person.

"Custis! What's the matter in there!"

Longarm backed out of the stall and closed the gate behind him. He had a sick feeling in the pit of his stomach that Matt's brother Joe was also dead. Miranda, meanwhile, had entered the livery, and when she saw Longarm's expression, her hand flew to her mouth.

"I want you to wait over here," Longarm said, leading the woman across the barn floor to a place near the door. Outside, the sky was turning a salmon color with sunrise.

Longarm made a quick search of the entire livery, and he found Joe's body covered with hay, his throat also cut wide open. Like his brother's, Joe's body had been searched and robbed.

"Miranda," Longarm said, "I'm afraid that Matt and his brother were both robbed and murdered sometime last night."

"Oh, my God!"

"We'll need to report this, of course, and get an undertaker out here as quickly as possible."

"I don't think that there is one in Cortez," she told him. "And it's probably too small to have its own marshal."

"Then the nearest one will be in Durango," Longarm said, thinking about Marshal Seth Palladin and wishing there were someone—anyone—else he could notify. The very last thing he wanted was to bring Palladin into this double murder.

"Let's get out of here," he decided aloud. "Let's just

take our horses and burro and ride on up to Mesa Verde."

"And leave them here like this?" Miranda cried, her face reflecting horror. "Custis, we can't do that!"

"We can't do a thing for them now," he said. "And while the murders appear to be robberies, that might not be the case at all."

"You mean—"

"I mean that someone might not want us to reach Mesa Verde and is doing whatever they can to discourage us. That's why I think we ought to just go on up while we still can. Someone will discover the bodies in an hour or two, and by then we will be well on our way."

"All right," she said, looking pale and shaken. "Let's just go!"

They saddled their horses, found the gear that Matt had collected for their trip, and lashed it down on their burro.

"We'll ride out the back way and then circle around south," Longarm said, anxious to be out of Cortez and on his way to the cliff dwellings.

"I can't believe that this happened," Miranda said. "Matt was so young and strong!"

"I know," Longarm said. "Whoever murdered him must have sneaked up behind him and killed him before he had a chance to fight back."

"This is horrible!"

"It could get worse," Longarm said. "Miranda, if you want, we could go back to Durango. I could put you on a stagecoach for Pueblo, and from there you could get to Denver."

"No! I'm not going to run out on you now."

"It would be the smart thing to do," he told her.

"Smart thing or not, the answer is still no!"

"All right then," Longarm said grimly as they pushed hard for the southern mesas. "We'll just have to find our own way up to Mesa Verde and, once we arrive, take our chances."

Chapter 13

The trail up to Mesa Verde was easy enough to follow, and two days later, Longarm and Miranda came upon their first Anasazi ruins.

"Would you just look at that!" Miranda cried with excitement. "It's so big!"

These were mesa-top ruins, and Longarm had read enough about Mesa Verde to know that the Anasazi people had lived and farmed up on the flat mesa centuries before building their famed cliff dwellings.

When Longarm and Miranda reached what appeared to be an ancient village made entirely of rock, logs, and mud, they dismounted and stepped forward to investigate.

"How big was this?" Miranda asked, looking up at the high rock walls. "And how old?"

"I have no idea," Longarm answered. "But it will be fun to have a look around."

The ruins were silent and overgrown with grass and even some pinyon pines, yet they were substantial and still impressive with their stairways, round ceremonial pits, and sturdy rock walls. Longarm was greatly impressed by the industry of a people who must have labored for generations to create these silent stone edifices.

"Come this way," he said, leading Miranda around a broken wall and then coming to the entrance of what appeared to be a corridor of small, dark rooms.

"I wonder how many people lived in this village," Miranda said, ducking through a narrow doorway into the series of connecting compartments that were less than ten feet square.

"I would expect at least a hundred people once lived in this place," Longarm said.

Miranda craned her head back. "Look how solidly they built their roofs. Why, I bet horses could have ridden over them and not fallen through."

It was true, even if these people had lived in this place long before the Spanish conquistadors first brought horses to North America. The light was poor, but Longarm could see that the Anasazi had used logs to cover their rock-walled compartments, and then had filled in the roof cracks with mud mixed with leaves, grass, and bark, which had, in turn, been covered by a deep layer of rock and dirt. Most of the small rooms were connected by key-shaped doorways, which Longarm had trouble squeezing through because he was so much larger than the ancient ones who'd lived and raised their families there.

"I can almost *feel* their spirits," Miranda whispered, kneeling and brushing the floor with her fingertips. "And just look at these dirt floors. They are as hard-packed as if they were composed of granite."

Longarm ran his fingers down one of the old pine door frames worn smooth by the touch of countless hands over countless centuries. He inhaled deeply, feeling the aura of a long-lost people whose daily life he could not begin to imagine. Had they lived in these small, dim dungeons only during the coldest months of winter, and then lived outdoors the remainder of the year? Had each of these rooms had fires for warmth, and if so, where would the smoke escape and why weren't there soot marks on the ceilings? Were these cold dirt floors once covered with animal skins, and did laughter resound through these stone catacombs as children played, women worked, and men went out to hunt?

Probably.

Longarm marveled at the engineering and industry of these people. He did not expect to find artifacts because they would all have been picked clean by the discoverers and the first tourists. Yet he could not help but feel that, if he had but a few hours to spare, he could probe just a little here and there and be assured of making his own discoveries. Perhaps a burial site or a prized Anasazi weapon hidden in some crevice. Or a perfect piece of pottery such as he had seen at Laird's museum tucked secretly away into some yet undiscovered niche or cranny in the stone walls.

Miranda shuddered. "I don't understand why these people didn't build window holes for sunlight," she said.

"My guess would be that windows would have allowed more cold winter air and wind to get inside."

"You're probably right, but I need sunlight."

"There's a doorway in the next compartment," Longarm told her. "We can climb out there."

They exited into what Longarm guessed was once a second-story courtyard where women probably ground corn and prepared most of their meals. The enclosure was rectangular and about forty by sixty feet, sided by the crumbling remains of what had been third-story rooms. In one corner of the courtyard lay the ashes of a recent campfire, which Longarm judged to be a sad and irreverent reminder of his own far more acquisitive culture. The shards of broken whiskey bottles and the rusting tin cans made his lips curl with contempt.

"Plunderers," he said, pointing to a large and offensive hole in the courtyard that someone had recently dug in hope of finding valuable artifacts.

"It's a travesty," Miranda said, "that anyone and everyone can just come up here and begin digging and tearing up these ancient ruins."

"You're right. When I return to Denver, I'm going to see what can be done to get Mesa Verde federal protection. These sites ought to be preserved for future generations."

"I wonder if whoever dug this area up found anything especially valuable."

"I hope not," Longarm said, moving off to examine what he knew was called a kiva, an underground ceremonial chamber.

The kiva was impressive despite the fact that its roof had collapsed and the chamber was filled with rubble. Longarm could see the remains of what had once been a ladder. It was now rotted and broken, but still recognizable. A few minutes later, he climbed up to the pinnacle of a ruined tower, where he had a good view in all directions. Through the trees, he could see more ruins, and that made him realize that this mesa-top had probably served as the home for hundreds, perhaps even thousands of Anasazi.

Why, an archaeologist could spend his entire career up here discovering and excavating these ancient ruins, most of which must be hidden in these pinyon pine forests and buried just under the surface.

They spent more than an hour poking around in the ruins, and could easily have spent days. Miranda was especially excited when she found two very distinct petroglyphs where an ancient storyteller had once etched images of hunters and their quarry onto the surface of rocks.

"We'd better push on," Longarm suggested. "I've a feeling that there are dozens of sites like this to be explored. However, I really would like to see a cliff dwelling before it gets too dark."

"All right," Miranda said. "I wonder where our mysterious archaeologists are camped."

"I don't know," Longarm said. "From what I've learned, there are several mesas up here, all divided by deep, tree-choked canyons. It's in those canyons that we will find the cliff dwellings. I'd guess that's also where we're most likely to find the Harvard archaeologists."

"It's too bad that we didn't have time to get that telegram from Billy Vail that would tell us if they are legitimate."

"I'm sure Billy's telegram will be waiting for us when we return to Cortez. In the meantime, I think we'll be able to figure out if Barker and Lucking are pretenders or not."

They rode, seeing, and even passing close by, many crumbling ruins. Despite Miranda's protestations that they linger to explore the mesa-top for a while, Longarm insisted that they keep moving until they came upon the cliff dwellings.

"They'll be time enough to poke around up here once we find Cliff Palace and some of the other cliff dwellings," he assured her.

"There had better be," Miranda fussed, "or I'm going to be pretty upset."

"Well, I can't help that," Longarm said with asperity. "You know that I'm up here on official business."

"I know," Miranda replied. "But—"

"There!" Longarm said, pointing. "I'll bet anything that's the canyon where we'll see many of the cliff dwellings."

It was a deep canyon, perhaps a quarter mile across and filled with oaks, brush, and pines. Longarm could see a riverbed snaking along the bottom. It was dry now, but probably filled with water every spring after the snows melted. The sand-, copper-, and crimson-colored walls of this wild and majestic canyon were almost vertical.

"There is a trail over here," Miranda said. "It follows the rim south."

"Then let's keep our eyes peeled," Longarm told her. "We ought to reach the camp pretty soon."

A short time later, they intersected another trail, this one worn deeply by the hooves of pack animals, which Longarm figured were regularly supplying the archaeologists.

"I have a feeling that their base camp isn't far now," he told Miranda.

Sure enough, they came upon a spartan camp less than a half mile farther down the trail. There was a large tent, a crude table, two chairs, and a pile of wooden boxes and crates, but no scientists.

"Invited or not, we'll spend the night here," Longarm decided. "I expect that the Harvard people will return about sundown. In the meantime, I'll check out their camp."

"Are you just going to enter their tent and begin to snoop around?"

"Of course," Longarm told her. "Why don't you station yourself over there where that footpath leads to the edge of the cliff. I expect that's the head of the trail that leads down to Cliff Palace or some other cliff dwelling that these men are excavating."

"Do you think that—"

"Miranda," he said, "please just do as I ask. I'd like to be warned before they just pop into view while I'm rifling their belongings searching for incriminating evidence."

"All right," Miranda said. "But what do I do if they suddenly appear?"

"Holler out a greeting and block their progress just long enough for me to get back out in the open," Longarm instructed her. "That shouldn't be so difficult."

"Easy for you to say."

"Just tie our horses up and follow that trail to the rim. It shouldn't take me long to find out if these fellows are pirating artifacts or not."

"I'll bet the artifacts are going to Harvard University where they're supposed to go."

"I'll take that bet," Longarm answered, handing his reins to Miranda and hurrying off to search inside the tent.

In less than ten minutes, Longarm knew that Barker and Lucking were indeed members of the grave-robbing gang. Every crate was packed with skeletons and Anasazi artifacts, and there wasn't a scrap of paper or a single shred of evidence that linked these two men with Harvard University. Instead, he found several notes and letters that left little doubt that everything being packed off this mesa was headed for wealthy private collectors.

There were even several letters from wealthy collectors in Europe stating exactly what kind of Anasazi treasures they desired and the prices that they could pay for goods upon delivery to their countries.

Longarm was examining a collection of bows, arrows, and spearheads when he heard Miranda call, "Why, hello there!"

He quickly replaced the articles back into their packing crate, then carefully eliminated all evidence that he had been inside the tent and hurried back outside to sit on a rock and look bored.

Lucking was a big man in his early sixties with a gray beard and wire-rimmed spectacles. Barker was twenty years younger, of average height, and also bearded. Both men were trim and looked extremely fit, and very unhappy to see visitors, even one as pretty as Miranda.

"What are you doing in our camp?" Lucking demanded in a stern voice.

"We were just visiting," Miranda said. "We had no idea that anyone was up here, and when we stumbled onto your camp, we thought that it would be fun to wait and visit."

" 'Fun'?" Barker snapped, eyes boring into Longarm. "We aren't here to have 'fun'! We are archaeologists, and neither Dr. Lucking nor myself appreciates complete strangers moving into our camp."

"We didn't 'move into your camp,' " Longarm said, putting a little heat in his own voice to let these men know that he was not about to be cowed by their hostile behavior. "As you can plainly see, our burro hasn't been unpacked. My wife and I were simply hoping we'd discovered a friendly place to camp. However, I see that you are not hospitable."

Lucking had hurried into their tent, and Longarm

could hear the man opening some of the very same crates that he had just opened and searched. When Lucking emerged from the tent, he demanded, "What have you been doing here in our absence?"

"Nothing," Longarm said, trying to look as innocent as a child. "We've only just arrived, and I think that we will now be leaving. It's clear to me and my wife that while you may be scientists, you are not gentlemen."

He turned to Miranda. "Let's go, my dear. We certainly don't have to associate with these people."

"I agree," Miranda said, starting for her horse.

"Wait a minute!" Lucking said. "Perhaps we *have* been somewhat unsociable. I apologize. It would be acceptable if you camped here tonight. We have plenty of food, and even some after-dinner brandy."

Barker appeared to be shocked by the older man's offer. He started to protest, but Lucking ignored him and said to Longarm, "However, we will have to ask you to leave first thing tomorrow morning. Our scientific research leaves no time for social visits . . . as regrettable as that might sound."

"You're scientists?" Miranda asked. "How wonderful! Then I suppose that you can tell us *everything* about these ancient peoples."

Lucking smiled coldly. "I wish that were so, Mrs. . . ."

"Long. I'm Miranda and this my husband Custis."

"A pleasure to meet you both," Lucking said, glancing at his partner for a similar overture, but receiving instead a questioning frown.

"Why don't you unpack your burro and make camp over near the rim where it's flat," Lucking suggested. "John and I will tidy up things and start a cooking fire.

We have some delicious stew left over from yesterday. I hope that sounds good."

"It sounds great," Longarm said, only now realizing that they had eaten very little this day other than a few dried apples and biscuits. "We'll be back soon."

"Good!" the older man said before turning away to disappear inside the tent.

Longarm and Miranda made their camp about fifty yards from the pair, and Longarm explained to Miranda what he'd found in the tent. They took their time unpacking the burro and laying out their sleeping bags and food supplies. While doing that, Longarm could not help but be reminded of the murdered Horn brothers, and he wondered if this pair of impostors knew of their horrible fate. Probably not, for this was a very remote setting and Longarm doubted if anyone else was camped on this mesa.

"How are you doing, Miranda? Ready to play the ignorant dinner guest?"

"Not really," she told him. "Actually, I'm scared half to death. I mean, they are so *convincing*."

"Yes," Longarm said, "and it's quite possible that they actually are scientists who have simply chosen to trade their academic respectability for riches. We'll find out soon enough how much they really know about the Anasazi."

"Then you intend to question them?"

"Of course!" Longarm smiled. "At least enough to remove any doubt whatsoever as to their authenticity."

"But you don't know much about the Anasazi. How will you know if they are telling the truth or not?"

Longarm shrugged. "It's true that I don't know much about these people. But Miranda, it's also true that a skunk always smells a bit rank, even when he doesn't intend to smell. Believe me, I'll know if these fellas are simply con men, or if they really do have some scientific training. I'll know it right away.''

"And then?''

"Then nothing,'' Longarm said. "We just play the part of the dumb and happy newlyweds off on their honeymoon. Tomorrow, we'll go down into the canyon and visit a cliff dwelling or two, and then we'll hang around for a couple of days waiting for Mountain Packers to show up to collect the goods.''

"What if they don't come for weeks?''

"They will come a lot sooner than that,'' Longarm promised. "I know because the packing crates are all filled and the food is almost gone. These two here need to be resupplied right away.''

"What happens when Mountain Packers arrive?''

"I haven't decided yet,'' Longarm answered. "We could arrest the whole bunch on the spot, but I think I'd rather follow that pack string back down to Durango, see who is waiting to collect the artifacts, then who they are being delivered to elsewhere in this country before being sent abroad. That way, we can identify and arrest the entire gang from top to bottom.''

"It sounds pretty dangerous.''

Longarm gave Miranda a hug. "Don't worry, we'll just follow the pack train down to Durango. Then, if I have no other choice, I'll ask Marshal Palladin to help me make all the arrests.''

"I thought you held him in very low regard.''

"I do,'' Longarm admitted, "but his presence might save me from having to shoot the ringleaders and then doing a lot of explaining. I've found, over the years, that it's always a good idea to bring in the local law, even when they are inept and incompetent.''

151

"I see." Miranda kissed his cheek. "So, we just go over there for some stew and pleasant conversation?"

"That's right," Longarm said. "And try to look relaxed and happy. I don't want them to think that you've already decided you made a bad marriage."

Miranda managed a laugh. "Okay, I'll play the fool and try to keep my mouth closed."

"Oh," Longarm said, "you don't have to do that. I know that you've plenty of questions to ask of your own concerning the Anasazi, and I urge you to ask them. If nothing else, it should make for a very interesting evening."

"You're right about that."

A few minutes later, they strolled into the archaeologists' camp, where they were treated graciously by their hosts. If was damned odd, considering how hostile the pair had been at first, but Longarm saw no point in bringing up that fact.

"So," Longarm began, "you're here to learn the secrets of these ancient Indians."

"That's right," Lucking said, watching him closely. "Although I must admit, the secrets of the people who walked this mesa many centuries ago are still veiled by time and the elements. At best, my colleague and I will make a few minor discoveries before we are forced by winter to leave this mesa."

"We were fortunate enough to speak to Mr. Laird down at his museum in Cortez," Longarm said, "and I expect you probably know him."

"Laird?" Barker asked, looking quizzically at his partner. "Yes, isn't that the fellow that—"

Lucking wanted to change the subject. "We believe," he said, "that these ancient peoples lived far longer up on this mesa than they did in their cliff dwellings."

"What makes you think that?" Longarm asked.

"The extent of the ruins we are finding up here," Lucking answered. "For example, we find layers of civilizations one on top of another, indicating that when a structure burned down or was abandoned to the elements, it was later reconstructed and inhabited. We have also found a very sophisticated canal system that was used to channel rain and spring runoff throughout all the fields."

"What fields?" Longarm asked. "We saw no—"

"The fields," Barker said, "are now all long since overgrown with stands of juniper, pine, and gambrel oak. You have to understand that this mesa has been abandoned for about a thousand years, give or take a few centuries."

"Why was it abandoned?"

Barker was more than happy to give his theory, and it was about the same as what they had heard earlier at the museum. Basically, that Mesa Verde had probably been abandoned because of a protracted drought coupled with deforestation, resulting in a lack of winter fuel and a general debilitation of the soil, which would, as any present-day farmer now understood, fail after repeated plantings of the same basic crops.

"I can imagine that the demise of Mesa Verde's agriculture would have come about very gradually," Lucking said. "Probably so gradually that it caused families to relocate over a long period of time rather than a mass, organized exodus of the entire Anasazi culture."

"I see. Have you found many artifacts?"

"Oh, a few," Lucking said nonchalantly. "But that isn't our purpose here, and we leave most of them where they are discovered. We're scientists, not looters of an ancient civilization. We seek only to learn."

I'll bet, Longarm thought, while saying, "That's quite admirable. Will you return next spring to continue your research and excavations?"

"Certainly," Lucking assured them. "This is our fourth season up here, and we hope to return for many more years."

Sure you do, until you've gutted this entire mesa and become millionaires.

Miranda asked, "What can you tell me about Anasazi women? Were they, for instance, happy?"

Longarm almost clapped his hands, for the question was precisely the kind that some completely innocent and ignorant tourist would ask.

"Happy?" Barker repeated, glancing at his partner, then back at Miranda. "I don't know if it will ever be possible to answer that question."

"What is your own opinion?" Miranda persisted.

"I like to think that they *were* happy," Barker said, looking off into the darkness as if peering back across time. "The women would have had to work hard, of course, for their duties were to gather pinyon nuts in the fall, keep the cooking fires going all winter, and gather all the wood, as well as grinding corn and tanning hides and making turkey-feather robes."

"We saw one of those," Miranda said, "at the museum in Cortez."

"Yes," Barker said, "and they are remarkably warm. We find the bones of many turkeys in the rear of the cliff dwellings, and know that they must have served not only for feathers, but also, in times of famine, as a staple food supply. We have also discovered the bones of dogs, so we know that the Anasazi kept them as pets and probably as hunting partners, in addition to their value as sentries against enemies."

154

"Who were the enemies of these people?" Longarm asked, impressed by Barker's knowledge.

"We don't know that either," Lucking interjected. "But consider this. Any agrarian people would have kept food stores that would have been very attractive to a more nomadic people. The nomadic people are always the aggressors."

"How would they know that there were food stores?" Miranda asked.

"Very simple," Lucking answered. "There is no doubt that the Mesa Verde Anasazi were primarily farmers rather than hunters or even gatherers. Their population was far too large for wild animals to have sustained their numbers. And as farmers, they would have kept a good supply of seed for the following year's harvest. If it were lost, they would have nothing to plant and so would quickly perish of starvation."

"That makes sense," Longarm said. "Did they store their seeds back inside the caves?"

"Yes," Lucking answered. "We've discovered large bins of old Indian corn. It has all been eaten by rodents and birds that have gone up and under the cavern roof, but the cobs and the rinds from squash remain, giving us clear evidence that the Anasazi understood the great importance of storing large amounts of food during the good years for use during the bad."

"What would cause the bad?" Miranda asked.

"Rain and snowfall levels can vary considerably along the western slopes of the Rocky Mountains. In a good year with abundant water, the Anasazi harvest would be bountiful, unless there was an early frost. But without the precious gift of water, the harvest would fail to materialize. We think that these people stored several years' worth of winter food in their caverns. And that would have been a major incentive for their enemies to attack.''

"How could they attack anyone down in the face of a cliff?" Longarm asked.

"They would have had a very difficult time indeed," Barker answered. "To be sure, they would have had to attack during the most vulnerable time of the year."

"Which would be during the harvest," Miranda said.

"Precisely!" Barker exclaimed, looking pleased. "And so, because the harvest could be neither ignored nor shifted even by a week or two, the enemies of these people would know when the Anasazi would be most vulnerable to attack despite the inaccessibility of their cliff dwellings."

"There's a lot more to think about than first meets the eye," Longarm said. "A whole lot more."

"There is indeed," Lucking told them in his most professorial manner.

They talked for another hour before Lucking began to yawn and then excused himself, saying, "We get up with the sun and generally go to bed with it as well. Good night."

"Good night," Longarm said. He turned to Barker and asked, "When is your next shipment of supplies arriving?"

"What makes you—"

"Well," Longarm said, knowing he was skating on thin ice, "someone must bring supplies up here and pack out a few of your findings."

"Uh . . . yes. Let's see. I'm not sure that we will be supplied again this season. In fact, I rather doubt that we will. You see, we will be leaving this camp very soon."

"Of course," Longarm said, knowing full well that the man was a liar. "Good night."

"You *will* be breaking camp and leaving in the morning," Barker said, looking rather uncomfortable. "I mean, it is not that we don't trust you to be up here when we are down in the cliff dwellings, but . . ."

"We intend to climb down with you in the morning," Miranda said, "if you don't mind terribly."

It was clear that Miranda had caught Barker by surprise, and that he was none too pleased with the notion of them accompanying him and Dr. Lucking down into the canyon.

Before Barker could muster up an objection, Longarm said, "Of course he wouldn't mind, darling! After all, this *is* a free country and the cliff dwellings are for everyone to see and enjoy. Right, Dr. Barker?"

What else could the man do but nod his head and mutter, "Sure. You can follow us down. We're working in Cliff Palace. It's the biggest and most magnificent of all the dwellings, but I have to warn you that the trail down is very dangerous. One misstep and you could easily fall hundreds of feet to the rocks below."

"I think we can handle it, don't you, my dear?" Longarm said.

Miranda just stared at him with her eyes wide and fearful.

"Perhaps my wife would prefer to remain up here on top, and I will come down for an hour or two on my own," Longarm told Barker.

"Whatever you wish," the man said before disappearing into the tent.

After Miranda and Longarm returned to their own camp, she said, "What do you think?"

"Guilty as sin, but also extremely intelligent and

157

knowledgeable. I suspect that they really are archaeologists turned outlaws. It's a pity, but I can't offer you any other explanation."

"I'll have to think about whether or not I want to climb down some rock face to get to Cliff Palace."

"It's entirely up to you," Longarm said, "but I wouldn't miss it for the world."

Miranda took a deep breath, and he wondered what she would do early the next morning. Longarm also wondered if Lucking and Barker were suspicious and if he and Miranda had more to worry about than falling off the side of a high cliff.

Chapter 14

"Oh, my God!" Miranda cried when she peered over the lip of the canyon and saw the impossible trail that she would have to descend in order to reach Cliff Palace far below. "This is insane!"

It was early in the morning, and there had not even been time for breakfast, let alone a cup of coffee. Longarm had seen the two archaeologists pass their camp on the way to the rim just as the sun was breaking over the eastern mountains. It was clear that they had decided to slip away in the hope that he and Miranda would be discouraged from making the descent.

Well, it isn't going to work, Longarm thought. At least not for me, it isn't.

"Look, Miranda, why don't you just stay up here and keep the horses and our burro company while I go down and see the cliff dwelling. Maybe later we can—"

"Oh, no! I've been wanting to visit one of these places for years, and I'm not turning back now."

"Are you sure?"

"Yes."

"You'd better be," Longarm told her. "The last thing we need is for you to freeze up on the side of this cliff and then expect me to somehow help you back up to the top."

"Go first and I'll follow."

Actually, Longarm wasn't so sure that he wanted to try the descent either. However, if those two scientists could do it, then dammit, so could he.

"Here goes," Longarm said, starting over the top into a narrow fissure of rock. "For hell sakes, don't slip and fall on me or we're both goners."

"That's what you are *really* worried about, isn't it!"

Longarm didn't answer. It seemed impossible to him that the scientists could have descended this way, but he'd watched them do it. How the Anasazi had gone up and down here *every* day in all kinds of weather, carrying rocks, water, their harvest . . . well, it defied the imagination.

"There are toeholds dug into the rock down here," he called up to Miranda after he had crabbed his way down about fifty feet. "I sure hope that they don't require a special sequence."

"What do you mean, a special sequence?" Miranda called in a strained voice.

"I mean that it's going to get even riskier when we have to exit this fissure and crab across a sheer rock wall. It could be that I'm supposed to start with one foot or the other. That's the kind of thing that would discourage any enemy from attempting to enter Cliff Palace."

"This is crazy!"

"Oops," Longarm said. "Wrong foot. Miranda, put your *left* foot into the first toehold, and that way you'll end up properly after crossing this bad stretch."

"This is *all* a bad stretch!"

"Quit complaining," Longarm said, inching his way down through another fissure and feeling light-headed whenever he gazed down at the canyon floor far, far below.

"Couldn't we have used ropes or something!"

"No," Longarm said. "We didn't bring enough."

"I think I'm going to faint!"

Longarm glanced up at Miranda. She did look pale, and he could see that there was a shine of perspiration on her face despite a crispness in the morning air. "Don't look down," he warned. "Just keep your eyes on your feet and hands."

"My feet *are* down, dammit!"

"Take your time," Longarm said, praying that she would not fall and send them both to their deaths.

Miranda clung to the wall for several minutes, and just when Longarm was about to urge her to retreat back up to their camp and wait for him, she started down again. This time, he waited until she had traversed the section of toeholds and reached him.

"Too late to turn back now," he said.

"I can't believe that anyone could be stupid enough to do this—especially me!"

"It will be easier climbing back up," he said, trying to sound encouraging. "It always is."

"How could Lucking and Barker carry Anasazi artifacts up the face of this cliff?"

"My guess is that they probably fill a basket, then pull it up on a very long rope. I dunno. I didn't ask."

"I wish I were in a basket instead of clinging to the side of this rock like a damned spider!"

"Maybe the worst is past us," Longarm said. "Come on. The longer we sit here talking, the harder it gets."

Longarm continued slowly down the trail, and he was immensely relieved because it actually did become easier. In fact, the last stretch was very safe. Then they rounded a boulder and beheld Cliff Palace.

"Can you believe this," Miranda whispered, clutching his arm. "It's even grander than I'd imagined!"

Longarm was also in awe of the abandoned city that lay protected from the elements by a great limestone cavern every square yard of which was filled by apartments, elegant winding stairways, and neatly plastered walls. There were also courtyards, kivas, and well-preserved ladders that had once allowed the Anasazi to climb easily from one level of the city to another. When he craned his head back, he could see that the top was blacked by smoke from the fires of its ancient inhabitants.

"I never imagined it was so big and . . . and impressive," Longarm exclaimed. "Look at the stonework! The corners of every wall and building are perfect!"

"Can you imagine the heartache these Indians must have felt when they were forced to leave?" Miranda asked. "Especially after laboring so long and hard."

"No, I can't." Longarm heard the sound of a pick or shovel chipping at rock, and knew that the archaeologists must already be at work excavating. "Miranda, let's go see what our two friends are up to."

"They're not going to be very happy to see us."

"I know. I want to watch them for a while before we announce our presence."

"Good idea."

Lucking and Barker were down inside one of the great ceremonial kivas, and their grunts of exertion could plainly be heard in the silence of the ruins. The scientists had already brought up a number of bones and some large pieces of the gray pottery etched with black designs that were characteristic of the Mesa Verde Anasazi.

"What shall we do?" Miranda asked.

"Since they may be down there for several more hours, I suggest we take a tour of these ruins."

"I'd like that."

Longarm was not a superstitious man, but as they crept through the little rooms and admired the beautiful red and black designs on the inside walls of a bedroom, he could almost *hear* the whisperings of ancient spirits.

"It's cold here," Miranda said once as they ducked into what appeared to have been a storage room. "I bet the old people really suffered from rheumatism and aching bones."

"I suspect so," Longarm replied. "My guess is that they stayed very near the mouth of the cave and soaked in as much of the afternoon sunshine as possible."

"Do you think that quite a few of their children fell to their deaths?"

"I imagine the children must have learned quite young to stay away from the mouth of this cavern and that their mothers watched them like hawks."

"I hope so," Miranda said as they left the storage compartment and passed along a second-story balcony that connected two separate square towers. "Everywhere I look I see places where you could fall to your death."

"I doubt that they saw it that way," Longarm told her. "I'm sure that they felt right at home and very safe from all enemies."

Longarm and Miranda worked their way deeper into the cavern, back where they had been told that the Anasazi kept their domesticated turkeys penned and also deposited their refuse. Sure enough, they discovered evidence of turkey droppings as well as many bird and animal bones.

"I could spend *years* poking around in here, digging up things," Miranda said. "I wonder if the other cliff dwellings are as big as this one."

"I don't think so," Longarm said, looking back toward the kiva where the archaeologists were still working. "Cliff Palace is supposed to be the largest."

Just then, Barker and Lucking emerged, cradling dirt-crusted objects in their arms.

"What are we going to do?" Miranda asked as they ducked behind a wall.

"I think we ought to announce ourselves and take a look at whatever it is they are bringing out of that kiva," Longarm answered.

"But won't they become suspicious?"

"I don't think so," Longarm answered. "At any rate, I'm not one to slink around. Let's just greet them as if we were out exploring and having a good time."

When Lucking and Barker realized that they were not alone in Cliff Palace, they were less than friendly. Lucking was especially incensed.

"This is really no place for tourists without experienced guides," he said, giving them stern looks. "I would have thought that you would both have had more sense than to attempt that descent without a guide familiar with the trail."

"We are adventuresome," Longarm said, determined not to allow himself to be rankled. He glanced over at the partial skeleton and the newly unearthed pottery, some of which was unbroken and no doubt very valuable. "I see that you're not leaving everything you find in that kiva."

"We examine it and then *return* it!" Lucking

snapped. "And anyway, what concern is it of yours?"

"None at all," Longarm replied. "I'm all for scientific research. As long as it's well done and for everyone's benefit."

The younger archaeologist said, "These ruins can be quite dangerous to the uninitiated. You could fall through rubble and be killed. My suggestion is that you both leave and perhaps return next spring with an experienced guide."

"We don't need a guide," Miranda angrily retorted. "And neither do we need your advice."

"We have important work to do," Lucking said stiffly as he climbed back down the ladder into the kiva.

"Yes," Barker said, "if you'll excuse us."

"Sure." Longarm smiled disarmingly. "Just pretend that we aren't even here."

Barker gave him a cold look and then vanished, leaving Miranda and Longarm alone with the displaced artifacts.

"What now?" she whispered.

"We'll leave in an hour or so," Longarm told her. "I don't know about you, but the sooner I get up on top of the mesa, the better I'll feel."

They left Cliff Palace a short time later, and climbed back up to the top of the mesa without incident. They cooked a long-overdue breakfast and enjoyed a pot of coffee. The sun warmed them, and after their strenuous climb, it was easy to lie back and take a nap.

"Hey!" a voice called, bringing Longarm and Miranda out of a restful sleep. "Who are *you*?"

Longarm sat up and looked at a pair of cowboys who were standing about fifteen feet away. They looked friendly enough, so he said, "Hello."

"What are you and that woman doing up here?" the

cowboy repeated. "There ain't no guides around."

"We decided to come up without one," Longarm told them, not caring if it sounded foolish. "Who are you?"

"We work for Mountain Packers," the cowboy answered. "And we've just delivered supplies for Dr. Lucking and Dr. Barker. Are they down in the cliff dwellings today?"

"As far as I know," Longarm said, thinking what a great stroke of good luck it was to have these men here so soon. "Will you be staying a while?"

"Naw, we're going down tomorrow," the other cowboy said. "We work our pack string out of Durango."

"I see."

"Funny time to be takin' a nap," the taller of the pair remarked. "Why, it ain't even noon!"

"We're on our honeymoon," Miranda explained, rubbing her eyes and stretching with a yawn.

The cowboys suddenly looked embarrassed, and without another word, they marched back to their pack string of mules and began to unload supplies.

"What are we going to do now?" Miranda asked.

"I'd say that we ought to follow this pair down to Durango and see who is picking up those boxes of artifacts that I inspected yesterday."

"Good idea."

When Barker and Lucking returned to the mesa-top late that afternoon, they were anything but sociable to Miranda and Longarm, and did not invite them into their camp. That evening, the wind began to blow and the temperature plummeted.

"I'm afraid we might be in for a snowstorm," Longarm said, his expression grim.

"We could go back down into Cliff Palace and stay dry."

"We might never be able to climb out again given the snow and ice that could coat the cliff face."

"Then what are you thinking?"

"I'm thinking that we had better cross our fingers and pray that we can ride off this mesa first thing in the morning."

"Maybe Lucking and Barker will have to do the same," Miranda said.

"I expect that they will," Longarm answered. "It appears to me like this country is going to have an early and hard winter. I also can't imagine that they would be very happy about trying to climb up and down the face of that cliff when the toe- and handholds are filled with snow and ice. I'm sure that they'll have to pack up everything and come on down with the gents from Mountain Packers."

"That would work to our favor, wouldn't it?"

"You bet it would," Longarm said. "So let's see if we can keep from freezing to death tonight and cross our fingers that this is just a weak, passing storm."

Longarm moved their camp into the shelter of some rocks that offered a good deal of protection from the wind. He fed their animals grain, and made sure that they were well tied and could not break away if frightened by the storm. By the time he was finished, the snow was really starting to come down and it was very cold.

"We'll be fine," Miranda told him as he huddled beside their fire and tried to warm his hands. "These storms are usually fast-moving."

"Yeah," he said, deciding that he had better change into a dry shirt and pants before jumping into his bedroll.

Miranda had other ideas. As soon as Longarm was undressed and before he could reach for a change of dry clothing, she was kissing his chest, then rubbing his half-frozen thighs. "Custis, let's sleep together and create some good old-fashioned body heat."

Longarm wondered why he hadn't thought of that first. He helped Miranda undress, and then they pulled her bedroll over his and began kissing and rubbing each other to increase their circulation. In a few minutes more, they were making love beside the hissing fire. Miranda was more passionate than she'd ever been before, and she rode Longarm until his hips began thrusting and he filled her with his hot seed. Then, her own body spasmed and she slumped forward, gasping for breath and clinging to him tightly.

"There is something about a stormy night that really gets me excited," she confessed.

Longarm kissed her mouth, and then studied her lovely face in the firelight. "Maybe it would be better if this storm lasted a few days."

"Don't be silly. We're not prepared."

"We've got enough food and there is plenty of firewood around. We could even go find shelter in those ruins we first discovered up here on the mesa. We could pretend that we were ancient Anasazi."

Miranda giggled. "I doubt that their women would have been as wanton as I've just been."

"Don't be so sure of that," Longarm told her.

Miranda sighed, and they held each other tight as the storm continued to intensify and he wondered what tomorrow would bring for them all.

Chapter 15

There was a foot of snow on the ground the following morning when Longarm and Miranda finally burrowed out from under the rocks and gazed up at a cold and cloudy sky.

Longarm shivered, then glanced over toward the archaeologists' camp and exclaimed, "The sonofabitches are all gone!"

"Well, what time is it?" Miranda asked.

Longarm dug into his bags and finally located his pocket watch. "Damn," he swore, "I forgot to wind it before we went to bed."

"Can't you tell by the sun?"

"What sun?" he asked, peering up at the dark and ominous storm clouds. "Miranda, let's get dressed, break camp, and get down off this high mesa before it starts snowing again."

Miranda didn't have to be told twice. She and Longarm started pulling on every bit of dry clothing that they had available, and then Longarm went to saddle the horses. But the horses were gone! Only the little burro stood shivering in the pines where Longarm had left their animals.

"Sonofabitch!" Longarm swore with a mixture of anger and frustration.

He hurried over to where the archaeologists had been camped and quickly read the tracks. Sure enough, two of them, probably the packers, had taken his rented saddle horses. No doubt they'd have taken the burro as well except that it had broken free and they hadn't been able to catch it. With the snow on the ground, it was easy to see that the packers and the archaeologists had headed down the mountainside, probably less than two hours earlier. It might as well have been two days earlier because Longarm knew that, on foot and in this weather, there was no chance of overtaking them.

Discouraged and more than a bit anxious, he managed to catch and halter their burro, then lead the animal back to their camp. When he saw Miranda, he said, "I'm afraid that we are going to have to hike down from Mesa Verde. They've taken our horses, but at least—"

"They've what!"

"Now take it easy," he said, trying to put the best face possible on this disaster. "We've got the burro and his pack, so we can carry most all of the supplies we brought up here. We may get cold, wet, and damned tired, but we'll make it."

"Custis, how could they *do* such a low-down thing!"

"My guess is that the whole bunch of 'em are just bad, and maybe they were suspicious of us coming up here so late in the season," he said, finding it damned hard to keep the discouragement and bitterness out of his voice. "And they probably figure that they'll be on their way east with their precious artifacts long before

170

we get around to feeling like asking any more questions.''

"We're in big trouble, aren't we.''

"I don't think so,'' Longarm told her. "Not unless it starts snowing again.''

"The sky looks pretty bad,'' Miranda said, gazing upward.

"Then we'd better stop talking and get to packing,'' he told her. "We need to eat and then be gone within the hour.''

Longarm packed everything he could, while Miranda somehow found enough dry limbs and twigs to get their fire blazing. And despite the fact that neither of them had much of an appetite, they forced themselves to eat well, knowing that the long walk down to Cortez was going to require all of their energy.

"Okay,'' Longarm said when they were finished and the burro was packed to its limit. "Let's get off this high mesa.''

They took off, following the tracks of the archaeologists and their packers. The snow was well tramped down, and it made the going a lot easier than if they had to break a fresh trail. Longarm took the lead dragging the burro, and Miranda brought up the rear. They hiked steadily all through the morning and stopped to eat at noon, then pushed on until darkness.

"We're real lucky that the weather is holding for us,'' Longarm said that night when, completely exhausted, they made their camp in the shelter of a stand of juniper pines. "But it just might storm again tonight.''

"It doesn't look good, that's for certain,'' Miranda said, gazing up at a night sky without a trace of the moon or stars.

Even the burro was discouraged, and was inclined to bray forlornly into the frosty air.

"Just one more day," Longarm said after they had eaten a cold supper and climbed into their bedrolls, hugging each other tightly for warmth. "One more day of clear weather and we're out of this mess."

It snowed again that night, and the wind was blowing hard when the first gray light of a frozen dawn appeared. By then, Longarm and Miranda had been awake for quite some time, but there was no sense in climbing out of their bedrolls and freezing in the darkness.

"Let's skip breakfast and eat some cold biscuits and beef," Longarm said. "I sure don't like the look of that sky to the north."

"Me neither," Miranda said. "And I expect that the tracks we are following will vanish in the blowing snow."

"Yeah," Longarm said, "but we know that they're either headed for Durango or that museum in Cortez. Either way, we'll catch them tomorrow."

"I sure hope so," Miranda said. "And after what they've done to us, I'd prefer to kill them all myself!"

"I'm afraid that you'll have to wait in line, darling."

By mid-morning, the wind was fierce and the tracks they had been following had been wiped away. With their coat collars pulled up under their chins and with the snow biting at their eyes, they had a brief discussion and decided to head for Cortez, simply because it was closer and they were getting weak from the cold and the effort it took to buck the bitter head wind.

At noon, Longarm unpacked the burro, fed it the last of their oats, then lifted Miranda up on its back and said, "You just hang on tight and enjoy the ride."

She was so weary that she could hardly force a smile.

"We haven't all that much farther to go, have we?"

"Just a few more miles and we'll be in Cortez, and then we'll get a room and have a hot bath and supper with whiskey and wine. How does that sound?"

"Heavenly. But what about—"

"We'll worry about catching up with them tomorrow morning," Longarm told her. "No one is going anywhere in this stormy weather, so we might as well enjoy ourselves for at least this evening."

"I couldn't agree more."

Longarm had hoped that they might meet a wagon or perhaps even a stagecoach that would bring them the last few miles of their exhausting journey down from Mesa Verde, but they had no such luck. And it was a good bit farther to town than he'd been willing to admit to himself, and so they didn't reach Cortez until just before nightfall. By then, Longarm was staggering and the damned wind hadn't let up at all.

They left the burro in a stall at the livery, which was now being run by a townsman, who had temporarily replaced Joe Horn, and hurried to the Concord Hotel. Jenny McAllister had a fit when she saw what poor shape they were in.

"My God!" she cried. "What happened!"

"It's a long story, ma'am. Could you have a steaming bath brought up to our room and later a good hot meal?"

"Why, of course! You both look like death warmed over."

"I'm sure we do," Longarm said, feeling his lips crack as he tried to smile and show that he was still game. "But we'll be much better by morning."

"Did you *walk* all the way down from the mesa?"

"I'm afraid so."

"In this terrible weather?"

"Wasn't any choice, ma'am. No choice at all."

"Let's get you upstairs to a room and we'll have that hot bath ready in no time."

"Thank you," Miranda said, her voice thin and trembling with weariness.

"My land," the woman said, "I sure wouldn't be going anywhere else with this fool!"

Longarm might have thought the remark somewhat humorous had he been in his normal good spirits. But as it was, he found himself entirely lacking in humor as he took Miranda's arm and steered her toward the stairs.

They soaked long and ate well that night, then slept like the dead, and did not awaken until almost ten o'clock the following morning.

"I'm feeling a lot better," Miranda told Longarm as he dressed and checked his weapons. "And I'd like to go out with you this morning."

"I'd prefer that you stayed in bed and rested," he said. "I doubt that our friends are in town anyway."

"But you said it was just as likely they'd head for Laird's museum as for Durango."

"Well," Longarm said, not wanting to place Miranda in any danger, "I changed my mind. I'm quite sure that they've gone to Durango."

"Then what—"

"I want to go to the telegraph office and see if I've heard back from Billy Vail on those two archaeologists," Longarm explained. "My guess is that Harvard University has never heard of either man."

"And then what?"

"I'll go pay a visit to Laird and ask him a few more questions."

"Will you arrest him?"

"Not yet," Longarm told her. "Not until we first arrest Lucking and Barker. Laird can wait a while longer. I'm sure that he isn't the leader of this bunch, and I don't want to spook them into hiding."

"Be careful," Miranda pleaded. "And if I can—"

"You can't," Longarm said. "Just stay here and rest up. We'll be heading for Durango the minute I can find a way to get there safely."

"All right."

Longarm went downstairs. He would have loved to have breakfast and hot coffee, but he felt compelled to seek out Laird and perhaps, if his hunches were correct, even catch Lucking and Barker at the museum unloading their last shipment of Anasazi artifacts before the pair headed east into a winter hiding.

The telegram that he was hoping for had arrived in Cortez several days earlier, and it read:

HARVARD HAS NEVER HEARD OF EITHER IMPOSTER
ARREST THEM AT ONCE BILLY

That telegram was all the reason he needed to approach the museum from its back side. Longarm drew his gun and eased up to a grimy rear window, then rubbed it clean and peered inside. A big smile creased his face, causing his parched lips to crack and bleed again. But Longarm didn't care because it was his good fortune to see not only Lucking and Barker, but also the two employees of Mountain Packers as well as Laird. They were sorting through the latest delivery of new artifacts, and so absorbed in their business that Longarm had no trouble getting the drop on them.

"Good morning !" he shouted, his gun trained on all five men who were crouched over an Anasazi mummy

175

that they had just removed from a packing crate. "Nice stuff, huh?"

One of the cowboys foolishly reached for the gun on his hip, and Longarm drilled him through the forearm. The man screamed and collapsed to his knees, wringing his bloody arm.

"Anyone else interested in losing the use of their arm . . . or worse?"

No one was. Longarm had them lie down on the floor and then, one by one, he used the same rope that had bound the packing crates to hog-tie his prisoners.

"We demand to know the meaning of this outrage!" Laird shouted.

Longarm extracted the telegram and read it out loud. "What this means, gentlemen," he said, specifically addressing Lucking and Barker, "is that you have been lying to everyone about your true intentions, which are to loot Mesa Verde cliff dwellings and realize enormous but illegal profits from the sale of their artifacts."

"You're crazy!" Lucking choked, his face apoplectic with rage. "And I'll see that you pay for this mistake!"

"Fine," Longarm told the man. "But that will have to wait until we reach Durango and I arrest your boss. Do you want to tell me who is he now . . . or must I get that information the hard way?"

"Go to Hell!" Barker hissed through clenched teeth. "You don't have anything on any of us."

"You're dead wrong about that," Longarm said, going over to extract a skull from one of the crates. The skull had parchment-like skin over its face and strands of long black hair. It was one of the best-preserved Longarm had ever seen, but also one of the most hideous.

"Isn't this one something, though," he said, turning

the skull one way and then another while his eyes shifted back and forth across his five captives seeking a look that would tell him who among them would be the most disgusted by what he intended to do next.

It was definitely the youngest of the mule skinners who had been supplying Lucking and Barker. Longarm read his revulsion, and went over to the bound man and pushed the Indian skull right into his face. The skinner went mad with horror, shouting and trying to jump up and run. Longarm put a knee squarely between the man's shoulder blades and said, "Maybe you'd like to—"

"No! Get it away from me!"

"Who is your Durango boss? Who is he!"

The other four hostages started shouting at the young man to keep his mouth shut, but the kid was oblivious to everything except the Anasazi skull that Longarm was waving before his round, panic-filled eyes.

"It's Marshal Palladin! He gives the orders!"

Longarm retracted the skull and studied the kid. There was no possibility that he was lying. "Thanks. I can't think of anyone that I'd rather arrest than that rotten sonofabitch."

"What about us!" Lucking cried.

"Oh," Longarm said, "I'll find a safe place to hold you until the weather clears. Then we'll go to Durango together, where I'll arrest Palladin and put you all on a stage for Pueblo, then a train for Denver. I'm afraid that you might have some difficulty adjusting to prison, but that can't be helped."

"You rotten sonofabitch!" Lucking cried. "I'll see that you pay for this!"

Longarm's stomach growled, reminding him that he needed a hearty breakfast. And so, after double-checking to make sure that the five were securely bound and had no chance of escape, he closed the door of the museum behind him and went off to have a good meal of bacon, eggs, and pancakes.

Chapter 16

The storm lasted for two days, and Longarm kept his captives hog-tied in the near-freezing museum the entire time while he and Miranda recuperated. When a warm chinook wind came and quickly melted the snow, Longarm hired an honest and willing freighter to take them all to Mancos, where they spent the night, and then to push on for Durango.

"I want you to pull this wagon in behind the livery and watch over these boys while I pay Marshal Palladin a surprise visit," Longarm told the driver when they neared Durango.

"Now wait jest a minute!" the freighter said, shaking his head back and forth. "I ain't no lawman. You paid me to—"

"I'm deputizing you," Longarm said. "And you'll be pleased to know that emergency pay for a deputy is five dollars a day."

"Five dollars?"

"That's right," Longarm said, making all this up. "I'll pay you three dollars now and two more in about another fifteen minutes when I return with Seth Palladin.''

"Well, hell, I'll do that for five dollars.''

Longarm paid the man three and then said to Miranda, "I'd rather you stayed here and kept an eye on our prisoners.''

"I'd rather come along with you just in case something goes wrong.''

"Nothing is going to go wrong, Miranda.''

She showed him her pistol. "I know, but just in case.''

"All right. As long as you stay out of harm's way.''

"Fair enough.''

Longarm headed for the jail, where he expected he'd find Palladin. However, when he got there, the man was gone and the office was locked.

"You lookin' for the marshal?'' an old-timer sitting in a rocking chair asked.

"That's right.''

"He's over at the saloon. Likes to have a shot or two of whiskey in the middle of the afternoon.''

"Which saloon?''

"The Lucky Dog just up the street.''

"Thanks.''

"You better not let that pretty woman go in there or you're just asking for trouble.''

"Miranda, you heard the man. I want you to wait on this side of the street and pretend to be looking in a shop window or something.''

"All right. But I can shoot straight and—''

"Just let me do this alone and we're on our way to Pueblo and then to Denver.''

"Do we have to go back home so soon?''

"I'm afraid so.'' Longarm relaxed a moment. "But I

promise that I'll take you on a hell of a nice vacation starting next week.''

That satisfied Miranda, and she stayed behind as Longarm angled across the street, making a beeline for the Lucky Dog.

When he reached it, he took a deep breath and stepped inside. Seth Palladin was easily the biggest man at the bar, and he was engaged in conversation when Longarm walked right up behind him, drew his gun, and said, ''Marshal, you are under arrest for the illegal theft and transportation of Anasazi artifacts. Put up your hands!''

Palladin swung around with his glass of whiskey and tossed it into Longarm's eyes, momentarily blinding him. Longarm's gun went off, but he missed, and the side of his face went numb from Palladin's fist. His knees buckled, but he lashed out with his pistol and managed to hit Palladin, probably saving his life as they fell to the floor. Palladin was trying to tear his own six-gun from its holster, and he almost did, but Longarm got a grip on his wrist and butted him in the nose with his forehead. It hurt, but not as much as it must have hurt Palladin, because the crooked lawman's nose broke and bled profusely on them both. However, just when Longarm was starting to take command, someone struck him in the back of the head.

''Miranda!'' he shouted, trying to cover the back of his skull from another blow while fending off Seth Palladin.

Miranda came charging through the door like the cavalry going to the rescue, and Longarm heard her gun bark, and then he heard a man shout in pain. He sledged Palladin in his broken nose again and again.

''Custis, stop! He's finished!''

Longarm climbed to his feet. He saw a man slumped

to his knees trying to plug up a bullet hole in his shoulder. Palladin was writhing on the sawdust floor, both hands covering his broken nose.

"Custis, are you all right?" Miranda asked, rushing to his side with a smoking gun clenched in her fist.

He felt wetness at the back of his head and a rising bump where the man with the bullet in his shoulder had slugged him.

"No," he said, "but I will be by the time we reach Denver."

"We got them all, didn't we?" Miranda said, the barrel of her six-gun shifting back and forth between Palladin and the one she'd shot.

"I'd say we did, or at least the worst of them," Longarm answered as he dragged himself to his feet and shouted, "Bartender, your best whiskey for me and my lady!"

"Yes, sir! Coming right up!"

He and Miranda had three straight shots before Longarm sent for a doctor to take care of Palladin and his wounded friend. Then, taking the bottle, they led the pair at gunpoint back to join the other members of the gang.

"Driver," Longarm said, handing the freighter two dollars he was owed, "how would you like to earn another five dollars a day *plus* a twenty-dollar gold piece as a bonus for delivering us to the train station at Pueblo?"

The driver gave him a big, toothless grin, spat tobacco juice, and said, "Marshal Long, it would be my pleasure."

Custis took another pull on the bottle of whiskey before he hog-tied Seth Palladin and his friend and helped them into the wagon with the rest of the gang.

"Let's get out of here," he said as a crowd of curious

locals started to gather. "It's just a damn sorry thing when a town has to see its own marshal whipped, arrested, and hog-tied."

"I have a feeling that Durango will be a whole lot better off finding a new marshal," Miranda told him.

Longarm nodded, and even managed a grin because he knew that his woman was not only brave and beautiful, but exactly right.

Watch for

LONGARM AND THE NEVADA NYMPHS

240th novel in the exciting LONGARM series
from Jove

Coming in December!